CHASERS

The Alone Series by James Phelan

Chasers
Survivor
Quarantine

atom

CHASERS

ALONE

JAMES PHELAN

www.atombooks.net

ATOM

First published in Australia in 2010 by Hachette Australia Pty Limited
First published in Great Britain in 2011 by Atom

Copyright © James Phelan 2010

The moral right of the author has been asserted.

A CIP catalogue record for this book
is available from the British Library.

ISBN 978-1-907410-67-3

Printed in the UK by CPI Mackays, Chatham ME5 8TD

Atom
An imprint of
Little, Brown Book Group
100 Victoria Embankment
London EC4Y 0DY

An Hachette UK Company
www.hachette.co.uk

www.atombooks.net

For my parents

From childhood's hour I have not been
As others were; I have not seen
As others saw; I could not bring
My passions from a common spring.
From the same source I have not taken
My sorrow; I could not awaken
My heart to joy at the same tone;
And all I loved, I loved alone.

Extract from 'Alone' by Edgar Allan Poe

then . . .

I missed home, that Australian heat, the laid-back people, the peace and quiet. Here, it was colder than I'd thought possible and everyone was in a hurry. Back home, I knew my mates would be hanging out at backyard barbies and playing cricket in the street, laughing and joking and vying to get each other out.

Maybe with time I'd get used to this place – who knows? All I know is that Manhattan is vast, too big for me to ever really feel comfortable in. It's as if the city has an entire country stuffed into it and is slowly being swallowed up, like that snake that eats itself. Ouroboros? I think that's what it's called. If I had to sum this place up for someone I'd say: *New York City, home to millions of people, endless city blocks, snow dump'n clouds, crowds that never stay still, consuming itself.* Too busy, too lonely, too much for me.

'What's the matter, Jesse? Never been on a subway before?' Dave asked. He was a big guy for sixteen, or at least big compared to the rest of us. His name might have been David but next to me he was more like Goliath. Dave and I had got on okay at the start of the camp, but right now I wished he'd put his foot in his mouth and start chomping, like Ouroboros.

'No, why do you say that?' I shifted my focus away from the guys in the middle of the carriage, who may or may not have been wearing gang colours and may or may not have been packing heat. I tried to look more confident, and smiled at the thought of Dave eating one of his stupid running shoes.

'You look a little nervous,' Dave said. 'Don't they have subways where you're from?'

'Yeah, but we don't call it that,' I replied. 'It's small – just a few stops in the city.'

'Everything must be small where you're from, huh?' Dave said, grinning. His perfect teeth were blindingly white against his dark skin.

'Where's that again?' Anna asked. She turned to look at me, flicking her shiny black hair over her shoulder. Anna's English but her parents are from India, and for a moment I was lost in her long eyelashes and bright red mouth.

'Melbourne . . .' I said. Dave's comment had just hit me – he thought I was small. I was kinda tall for my age back home, but yeah, I'm slight. It's just that I haven't quite filled out yet. I was torn between launching a comeback and trying to look unfazed in front of Anna. We're all sixteen, but she seems older, more sure of herself. I stood up a little straighter and tried to push my chest out.

'So, what is it then, Jesse? Never been on the subway without your mom?' Dave pushed. I wondered what his problem was. We'd been getting along so well until today. Maybe we were just getting cabin fever, which always seemed to happen on camps – sooner or later you'd get sick of your friends.

'Leave it,' Mini said in her quiet voice.

He looked from me to her, annoyed.

'I don't have a mum,' I said. The three of them stood in silence then. Looked at each other and then at the wet floor. That was always a conversation stopper. And it was mostly true. Okay, I *did* have a mum out there somewhere. And a step-mum back in Melbourne. But Barbara was a dragon and for all I knew my real mother might be dead.

5

'I've got two,' Anna said, like it was as natural as saying I've got *a* mum.

'Huh?' Mini asked.

'Carol and Megan.'

'How does that work?' I asked, then realised as soon as the words were out of my mouth. 'Oh, right, I get it. That's cool, I guess.'

'Trust me, you're not missing out on much.'

'Not at all,' Mini added.

There was a bit of an awkward beat and I wondered if maybe I shouldn't have said anything. I tried to think of a joke to lighten the mood, but I didn't know any where *having* a mum was the punch line.

'Check out the others,' Dave said. He was at least a head taller than us and had a clear view. The rest of our group were packed like sardines in the next subway carriage, a sea of light-blue parkas. As I looked, I tried not to make eye contact with the guys who may have been gang members. They were already on the subway when we'd got on at Grand Central, near our hotel and the UN, but I doubted they were headed to the 9/11 Memorial like us.

'They definitely don't look like the brightest sixteen-year-olds from around the world,' Anna said dryly. She was right. Like the four of us, they looked like total geeks, wearing blue plastic parkas with white *UN* lettering on the back, and *UN Youth Ambassadors* on the front left pocket. They stood out about as much as the gang members closer to us, as if we all wore colours as labels of who we were.

'Guess they won't get lost in a crowd,' I said. Mini laughed. She had this quiet, deep laugh that seemed odd coming from such a small package – the kind of laugh that was contagious. 'They're really getting into the spirit of togetherness.'

Beside the gang members there were only half a dozen other people in our carriage, the last of the train. It was just before midday and in between rush hours, so there were more tourists on the subway than commuters.

'Bet it really stinks in their carriage,' Anna said, her eyes fixed on the glass doors ahead. Mr Lawson, one of our UN minders, clocked us and started to head for the interconnecting doors. 'Like my brothers' rooms with all their dirty wet socks after football.'

'I don't know about you guys, but I'm gonna commute to work via helicopter when I'm older,' Dave said.

'What, are you gonna be a traffic reporter?' I said. The girls laughed.

'Nah, I wanna work for the UN,' he said, 'like my grandpa.'

'They had the UN back then?'

'Only I want to be out in the field,' he said, ignoring my remark. 'The front lines, relief work, disaster zones. Really get things done. What about you guys?'

'Teacher,' Anna said straightaway. 'In India. Start up a school for kids in poverty. There's millions and millions of them and they have nothing, nothing at all.'

I'm sixteen; I had no idea what I wanted to be, and I certainly didn't have a prepackaged beauty-pageant answer ready. Dave and Anna looked at me but I just shrugged. They turned to Min Pei.

'I don't know either,' Mini said. 'Maybe a doctor or a vet. Or an artist. Or maybe I'll marry money and do nothing. That would be cool.'

'I'm not sure if that's how it works, Min,' I said. I could see Mr Lawson was almost at the interconnecting doors, but to get to us he'd have to push through the gang members and half a dozen tourists; we were right at the back of the carriage. Beyond the door at our end was the darkness of the tracks as we rattled south towards Lower Manhattan. Mini looked through the window in silence. I saw her face reflected in the glass and realised she wasn't watching the tunnel disappear behind us – she was watching me. We locked eyes for a second and I felt myself going red.

'Think they live by the Golden Rule?' Mini asked, nodding towards the gang members.

'Sorry, Min?' Anna said.

'You know, that graffiti we saw when we did the city tour?' Mini said. 'You think those guys live by that?'

'Yeah, sure,' Dave said. *'Treat others how you want to be treated.* Yep, I'm real sure that's their creed.'

'Did we see that on some graffiti, or a mural at the UN?' Anna asked. We all thought about it and shrugged – even Dave, who had a memory like a bank vault.

'Let's just not bother them and they won't bother us,' I said. I noticed one of the guys had a massive gold crucifix hanging around his neck. Maybe they did have rules – maybe they were some kind of cool hip-hop priests? I doubted it, but I hoped they weren't as much of a threat as we were making them out to be.

'So, I got a joke,' Dave said. 'What do you get when you get a teenager from Australia, England, China and the US, and put them in a subway?'

Anna rolled her eyes.

'I'm not Chinese, I'm Taiwanese,' Mini said.

'What's the difference?'

'What's the difference between you and a Canadian?'

'Ouch, all right,' Dave said. 'Taiwanese, then. Okay, what do you get?'

'A boring trip?'

'Sore feet?'

'A growing contempt for American humour?'

Dave didn't seem put off.

'No,' he said. 'You get—'

There was a loud noise and our train shook so violently that we had to reach out to grab the handrails. Before I could say anything it happened again, the carriage tilting wildly sideways, creating sparks in the darkness outside. Mini fell next to me and I crouched down to help her up. We heard screams and shouts from the other end of the carriage as people spilled from their seats.

Mini and I stood up slowly. I must have hit my head on something when the train jolted because when I touched my eyebrow my hand came away covered in blood.

'Oh my god, are you okay?' Mini asked.

Anna pulled tissues from her backpack and told me to keep pressure on the cut. In the flickering lights of the carriage the gang guys didn't look so scary anymore. In fact, they were wide-eyed as they helped a tourist to his feet and stared back at us – no, behind us.

The hairs on the back of my neck prickled as I turned around and looked out the back window.

chasers

A massive fireball was chasing the train – it was only twenty metres behind us and closing fast. I yelled at the others to get down and reached out to Anna. By the time the four of us were on the floor, the subway carriage was rocked again, this time going off its rails and tipping on its side. There was a tearing screech of steel on steel and squealing and screaming and a whoosh of fire, and everything went from hot to black in a second.

now . . .

1

All I saw was darkness. I wondered if my eyes were open. It might have been some awful dream but I knew it wasn't. I felt pain, I felt pressure. I felt alone. I couldn't hear, but I knew there were sounds out here, around me. I was not alone.

A hand brushed my face, the fingers soft but probing in the dark. Purposeful, searching. It took me a second to realise it was my own hand, and it came away from my face wet and sticky. I felt a hot sharp pain above my left eye. I blinked but everything was pitch black.

Light erupted in a shower of sparks at the same moment the rest of my senses returned. There was an acrid, copper taste in my mouth and I could smell smoke. I tried to get up but something heavy was pressing against my back. I tunnelled backwards on my stomach, groped around in the dark—

A light shone in my eyes but I was even blinder than before. I saw stars and it hurt my head, like the light was hitting the inside of my skull and bouncing around in there. As my vision cleared I saw a tangle of—

Jesse!

I heard one of the girls call my name. I was helped up from the ground and in that motion I was suddenly awake, like the blood was pumping again and I had snapped out of whatever trance I'd been under.

Anna was there, her torch pointed at me, the light making me dizzy – and I saw Mini by her side. Dave was propped against the roof of the subway carriage, which I now realised was on its side. It was dark in the train, like we were in a cave or the belly of a monster. By the weak torchlight I could see my friends looked pale and frightened but otherwise seemed okay. There was another shower of sparks that ended with a small explosion and I saw what was left of the carriage ahead.

The others? I said.

Dave shook his head.

I swallowed some vomit. Started to shake.

How did this . . . ?

Some kind of accident, Dave said in a low voice.

We must have hit something and derailed. I can't see far into the carriage in front of us – can't see much of anything.

There was fire though, Anna added. Fire, coming up behind us, remember? And then pounding noises, like banging . . . It wasn't an accident, more like some kind of explosion.

I could still hear the banging, like far-off pounding on a door. I remembered the fireball coming at us but it didn't make sense. What could catch on fire in a concrete tunnel? The fireball had chased us, licked at the end of the carriage just seconds before everything went black and the world had turned on its side.

I bet it was terrorists, Mini said. My friends told me this might happen in New York. There must have been a bomb on the train or at one of the subway stations – it was terrorists, I know it was.

It wasn't terrorists . . . Dave's voice trailed off, like he was trying to convince himself as much as us.

We've had that kind of thing in London, Anna said. We have to get out of here—

It's not terrorists, Dave said in a loud voice, trying to end the discussion.

If it *was* terrorists, there might be more attacks, Anna said. We have to go and warn everyone!

I heard our breathing, hard and fast and irregular. I took the torch from Anna and held it out in front of me. As the light arced around the carriage I saw tangled legs, then a couple of familiar faces – the gang members, their expressions frozen in vacant, disturbing ways.

We have to get out of here! Anna's voice was edgy, like she was trying not to cry.

Shouldn't we try to get to the others—

And what? Anna said. Sit with them while they die? Wait here for the next train to come along and smash us to bits?

I heard her take a deep breath before she spoke again: Look, there might be another fireball and we need to find help. Proper, emergency services kind of help. We have to leave.

No one moved or said anything. We were waiting – probably for someone to come and find *us*. But I knew that help could be a long time coming, especially if we were counting on there being other survivors on the train. Anna was right.

I shone the torch towards the end of the carriage, just a few paces from us. The door had been blown off its hinges and the tunnel beyond disappeared into darkness. But not compete darkness – there was a faint light further down the tunnel, a dim shaft of illumination.

Is everyone all right? I asked. I mean, can you all move okay? Do you think we could make it to that light?

The others followed my gaze towards the distant point in the tunnel. We watched the light for a few seconds and I wondered if it was an approaching train. It didn't change though, didn't move.

Looks like a spotlight, Dave said, like emergency lighting or something.

Maybe it's daylight, I said. It could be an access hatch to the street above or coming from a subway station.

I steadied myself with one hand on an upturned seat, then turned and shone the torch back up the carriage. The beam was pitiful – the torch was a small wind-up one we'd each been given in our UN pack on induction day.

My phone has no reception, Mini said behind me, her voice close.

It won't down here—

Shh! I cut Dave off and we were all silent. There was a noise. I moved forward a couple of steps, the torch beam creeping over the twisted bodies of the gang members. There was no sign of Mr Lawson. Beyond the bodies, the subway car was pinched shut, like the roof of the tunnel had come down on top of it. I felt sick. This wasn't a collision, no way.

One of the gang members moved. A twitch of a leg. A hand raised towards the light. A faint groan.

Oh my god, Mini said. I felt her bump in close behind me.

I traced the beam up the man's outstretched arm and saw a face covered with blood, eyes looking back at me, caught in the weak light. He blinked once, then slowly closed his eyes.

Stay, I told Mini. I moved up the carriage, supporting myself against the roof of the train and stepping over the bodies of the other gang members. As I bent down to feel the man's pulse, the torchlight swung across his body and I saw where his legs used to be and more blood, so much blood. By his side was a pistol – a shiny, steel automatic, mean-looking. My fingers left the cold skin of his neck and I moved back to the others as quickly as I could.

We need to head towards that light out there, I said.

Is he—

Yes, let's move.

Okay, Mini said. Dave planted himself by the door-opening at the end of the carriage and helped the girls out. He practically lifted them to the ground outside. I wondered if he had some kind of super strength that came immediately after accidents, like when parents are able to lift cars off their kids. I went last and almost fell after tripping on a railway sleeper. The torch beam shook in my hands.

We walked in silence down the tracks, shell-shocked, the smell of smoke becoming stronger the further we went. We kept a hand on each other as we moved through the darkness and I realised for the first time that the white UN lettering on our parkas was fluorescent. We were like an emergency crew, only we were trying to get *away* from the scene of an accident. The image of the gang member's staring eyes flashed in my mind but I pushed it away.

There, Anna said. We were standing under the source of the light – a manhole high above us, the cover blown off. Smoke from the tunnel wisped out. The grey wintry clouds seemed unnaturally bright.

Can I have the flashlight? Dave asked.

I'll light the way for you guys, I said. I wound the base of the torch's plastic handle and the beam instantly became brighter. I pointed it towards the tunnel walls until I found the ladder rungs.

Can you all climb up? Dave asked us.

Yes, we said quickly, almost in synch.

Dave led the way. Anna followed his big bulk, which blocked out the light coming from above as he exited the tunnel. I watched as he helped Anna out, then held the torch steady for Mini, directing the beam ahead of her hands so she could see.

When Mini had reached the top, I checked my watch in the light before putting the torch in my pocket. It was after 1 pm. I realised I must have been unconscious for about an hour back in the train. Why hadn't the others said anything? Had they been out of it too?

Jesse! Dave called from above. Hurry!

I grabbed the dusty steel ladder and climbed one rung at a time, concentrating on not letting go. Halfway up I felt so dizzy I had to stop. My head was pounding and the pressure in my ears was so great it felt like it might blow my head clean off.

Jesse, you have to hurry! Anna yelled down into the tunnel.

I was almost at the top when I felt strong hands reach down and haul me up by my armpits. I was pulled out of the darkness and onto the cold white ground. I sat with my legs splayed, in the middle of a Manhattan street. There was no traffic. All was quiet but for the construction noises in the distance, like a million people were building an entire city in a hurry.

The others were all squatting down, close to me. Anna's hand rested on Mini's shoulder. I felt snow falling, the light, soft flakes that made for good skiing. It had rained too, turning the snow to slush underfoot. I closed my eyes, letting the snow fall on my face.

Jesse?

I opened my eyes and suddenly understood why there was no traffic. Along the street were hundreds of cars crashed into one another, some with their lights and engines still on, the exhausts steaming in the frigid air. The street was closed off, in both directions, by massive pile-ups.

Jesse? Mini said again.

The others were all staring at a point further down the street. I followed their gaze and saw thirty or forty people huddled in a big group.

Should we go to them? Anna asked.

Dave shook his head. Look at them, he said. Look . . .

I watched the group. Most of them seemed to have their heads tilted up towards the sky. The rest were kneeling on the ground, as if they were looking for something or in some kind of prayer.

What are they doing? Mini asked. Are they . . . are they *drinking*?

The group shifted a bit and I saw they were crowded around a broken fire hydrant. Water was spurting into the air like a geyser and these people were standing underneath, their mouths wide open, trying to catch the water as it fell. Others drank from puddles on the ground.

Is that Mr Lawson? Anna said.

It was. He was walking towards us, his UN parka hanging off one arm. He looked different from the man we'd known; his eyes stared vacantly and he was coming towards us at a strangely rhythmical pace.

Mr Lawson! I yelled.

He didn't reply.

What's wrong with him? Mini said.

He was ten metres away, but he stared straight through us as if we weren't there.

Mr Lawson!

He stopped short before us, squatted down and with cupped hands drank from a puddle. His thousand-yard stare was fixed on the water.

Mr Lawson, are you okay?

Anna had moved to go to him when Dave pulled her back.

Oh my god! he said. Behind him. They're . . . they're—

I caught the look on Mini's face and the hairs on the back of my neck stood on end. I followed her gaze and saw, as if in slow motion, the scene that had my friends transfixed in shock.

Amongst the group of people drinking from the sky and the ground was another, smaller group, hunched over the dead bodies in the street.

Like animals.

In horror, I realised that their mouths were closed over the bare flesh of those bodies. They were *drinking* from them. They were drinking everything. Anything.

Then they saw us.

2

It was the fastest I had ever run. My arms and legs pumped hard and my plastic parka blew out behind me like a sail. I looked over my right shoulder and saw Dave there, with Anna beside him and Mini just behind. Beyond them were our pursuers.

But . . . Mr Lawson, Anna gasped.

He'll be able to look after himself, I said.

I jumped over a bench and turned right onto Seventh Avenue, trusting the others would follow me. My shoes slid out in the tight turn and I almost lost my footing, but somehow I kept it together. I let Dave and Anna take the lead and fell in next to Mini.

Come on, Min, you have to push it!

We picked up the pace together, then almost smacked into Dave and Anna as they came to a stop in the middle of the street.

Cars were all around us. Empty. Abandoned. Most were crashed, some still had engines running, some were in pieces. But that's not what had stopped us. Ahead, north along the expanse of Seventh Avenue, we had a clear view of the destruction.

Buildings were crumbled onto the street like they were made of blocks and some giant kid had pushed them over. I was wrong about the construction noises I'd heard earlier – it was the sound of *demolition*, the booming bang crash of large-scale demolition. Six or seven intersections ahead, the street was impassable to all but a mountain climber. The road was blocked by at least five storeys of dangerous rubble; jagged pieces of concrete and glass that would cut you up if you took them on. Small fires were everywhere, and the air was thick with smoke and dust.

Something clicked in my subconscious and I looked behind us. Something else wasn't right, something I hadn't been able to take in at first. There were *dozens* of office buildings in ruins. Paper was falling through the air like autumn leaves and I smelled smoke, dangerous acrid smoke, like burning plastic or tyres. There was a massive crater at the start of the street and a school bus had almost disappeared into it. The scale of it all was surreal, like a movie full of special effects. But this was real and it was all around me.

Then I noticed the bodies. Hundreds of them. Covered in ash and debris. They lay awkwardly in the street, like they'd dropped there from a great height. Most were in one piece. Most were face down.

Suddenly an explosion shattered the facade of a ten-storey building on the next block. A fireball belched out, consuming the cars closest to the building and setting off a chain reaction of exploding vehicles; a horrifying fireworks display that was snaking towards us like dominoes.

Come on! I yelled.

Dave pulled Mini hard and Anna was next to me as we made for the next block. I hoped we'd reach it by the time the cars—

Half a yellow taxi landed to my left with a deafening crash. The engine was a second behind and it bounced off the ground and cleared right over the top of us as we ran.

In that second I saw them. At least a dozen people, chasing us. They didn't seem to be fazed by the explosions that continued to ricochet down Seventh. Two ran towards a body that lay by the corner. Another went to a puddle in a crater and dipped her face in like she was snorkelling, her palms flat on the ground, holding herself so close to the water that her forehead was immersed.

I ran flat out, my heart beating loudly in my ears. Dave and Mini were next to Anna and me now, and we were closing on 40th Street.

Right! I yelled. Turn right!

We followed Dave and Mini around a pile-up of taxis and vans and crossed the street. To our left was a heap of charred bodies. I saw Mini turning her head to look and told her to keep watching ahead, keep running.

We turned the corner onto 40th and all seemed relatively calm as we ran along the footpath.

People! Anna shouted, pointing into the middle of the road.

Three men were helping one another walk, their blood-soaked clothes hanging from them like an image from a war movie. Three men sticking together, three men looking for help.

We should—

Keep running! I yelled as I spotted another group – a very different group – rounding a corner in pursuit of the men. I went to push Anna's backpack to stop her from slowing down, but she was off more quickly than before and we kept our pace as we ran ahead. I glanced back and saw our pursuers as they rounded onto 40th Street.

Which way? Dave yelled. He'd taken the lead and I could see him urging Mini to keep up with him.

What's ahead?

More of the same! he yelled. Cars and fires 'n' crap.

No, what street? We need—

I tried to read the street sign . . .

Sixth! he said. North or south?

I glanced up at the sky, looking for some kind of sign of what was going on.

Terrifying screams came from behind us, and we all slowed down and looked in spite of ourselves.

It was horrible. The chasers were upon the three wounded men, and they had them down on the ground—

North! I yelled.

Dave pulled Mini along so hard that he almost dragged her over the snow-covered road as we headed for the corner. Anna and I were close behind them. I heard Mini starting to make freak-out noises, but before I could call out to her I was hit full in the face.

The shock slowed me almost to a standstill. I couldn't see and I swiped my hand over my face to find a sheet of A4. We were in the middle of a massive paper storm; it was as if a whole office-load of A4 was being blown at us by a giant fan.

We moved on more slowly, having to push our way though the awful ticker-tape parade. At the end of the street we turned left onto Sixth Avenue. The paper hurricane behind us, we settled into a half-run up the street, my heart still pounding in my ears.

We should find some cover, I said. Try a landline phone . . .

The looks on the others' faces made me stop.

Bodies had been blown halfway through a shop window to our left, and at that moment I really thought one of the girls would snap. One of the bodies had a large, pointed shard of glass stuck right through the chest. The corpses were so close that we could see the blood and gore and god knows what else spilled all over the ground. Dave saved us then:

Come on, he said, in that deep, sure voice we'd heard so many times during the past week. Next block, there's an arcade, big old stone thing. The way looks clear from here.

He ran closest to the shop window, blocking out the view of the bodies for the rest of us. Our eyes shifted ahead again and we ran towards the next block. I imagined what it would be like in the arcade, hoping it would be warm and bright and there would be other people in there. That there would be phones and police and a nice lady making tea and coffee, and that the fire department would be on their way. I heard a siren in the distance and then thought I'd probably imagined it as we passed an upside-down police car, smashed against a massive wreck of vehicles at the intersection of 42nd Street.

It began to rain; hard, heavy rain that was too torrential to turn into snow on its way down. My shoes were soaked. I wished I'd worn proper trainers like Dave did every day. I remembered thinking earlier in the week that he looked stupid with his white trainers and blue jeans and button-down shirt. But now, as I looked at the back of his extra-large UN parka, I thought he looked like an emergency worker, the kind of hero a situation like this needed. Even the back of his big head with its closely cropped hair looked like it could belong to a guy I'd seen in disaster movies.

Up here on the right, Dave said.

We followed him across the road between the wrecked cars and onto the footpath. My head was throbbing and my chest burned. I let my mind wander as I followed the two UN parkas in front of me, my legs settling into a tired sort of rhythm. I could smell the hot chocolate they were making in the arcade. I might have heard gunshots, but if they were real they were far off.

We disappeared into a glass-fronted building and headed towards the middle of the arcade. It felt solid and safe, like a cave. We slowed down, then stopped, sucking in the deep breaths we'd not dared take outside. *In through the nose and out through the mouth*, I heard my football coach say. My hands were on my knees and I was doubled over, my mouth dry, my hair and body pooling water onto the white marble floor. Drops of blood dripped from my eyebrow and diluted in the water, swirling and blooming like red dye.

Are we safe? Anna asked.

She was standing, her posture as straight as ever, looking back at the entry doors. Mini took a puff of her asthma inhaler and I wanted to hug them both and say, *Everything will be all right*, but I didn't know if it was true.

Dave walked back towards the glassed entry and looked out at the street.

There's no one out there, he said. It's raining even harder now. Be difficult for anyone to see much.

We caught our breath for a minute and then I dragged a long bench seat against the doors so it would be harder for someone to get in. We walked deeper into the arcade but I wasn't taking in much around me; I was just glad we were no longer being pursued. I was glad it was quiet.

Mini made a squeaking sound and then began to cry. Really cry. She put her whole body into it, standing there, her hands at her face, shaking, sobbing, sucking in air like she couldn't breathe.

Shh, Anna whispered and wrapped her wet arms around Mini in a tight hug. I remembered what it was like to be that close to Anna. We'd been on our way back to the hotel earlier in the week when it started pouring. We'd taken shelter together – I'd pulled her under a deli awning and we'd huddled close and then she'd kissed me and it was hot and fast, but she seemed to forget about it as soon as the weather cleared.

Anna was still rocking Mini gently. It's all right, she said. You'll be all right.

I glanced over at Dave and saw he was looking at me with that big open face of his. The fear in his eyes was too real and I looked away; he couldn't give me the reassurance I needed.

We should fix that cut of yours, he said, pointing at my eyebrow.

I turned to look at my reflection in the glass storefront behind him. I nearly laughed – it was a lingerie shop, so my face, with blood running down from my eyebrow to my chin, looked like it was attached to the body of a mannequin, complete with pink lacy underwear.

Shit! Anna said, looking at me. I'd not heard her swear before, but it actually sounded distinguished when she said it, like her parents had sent her to a special elocution school back in London where the young ladies practised swearing in plummy tones.

I was about to ask her to swear again but she'd let go of Mini – who'd stopped crying and was staring at me with her mouth wide open – to go into the shop.

I'm gonna find a phone, Dave said and left us there.

Good idea, I said.

I watched as Anna rummaged through the drawers in the shop's front counter.

Anna, I think the changing room is out the back, not under that counter, I said.

Mini choked back a laugh and I was glad to see she was almost smiling now.

Pay phones are dead, Dave said as he passed us and disappeared into a health-food store.

Anna came out with a small white plastic lunch box with a red cross on the top.

Here, she said, passing the box for Mini to hold. All right, this might hurt . . .

She patted my bleeding forehead with a pair of scrunched-up knickers. They smelled of disinfectant and I watched her dab some more on from a small bottle as she worked to clean my face.

They're actually really soft, I said. Silk?

Mini laughed and Dave grumbled something about the internet not working as he went into the lingerie shop.

Don't think they have anything for you in there, Dave, I called after him. Unless you're into that sort of thing – ouch!

Anna pushed a fresh patch of soaked underwear against my cut and I could feel it bleeding under the aggravation.

Not that that there's anything wrong with that, I said, as Dave exited the store and headed deeper into the arcade.

All the phones are out! His voice echoed back at us.

Then why do some of these lights work? Anna asked as she dabbed at me some more. It was like she was pecking at me with the cloth, not gentle at all, the kind of rough job I could have done myself. My great-grandfather had fought in World War I at my age and I wondered if he'd ever had a British nurse like Anna: beautiful, painful, efficient and unobtainable.

It must be emergency lighting, I explained, as Anna held the underwear tight against my cut. See how only some lights are on?

I gestured to the dim fluorescent tubes in the ceiling.

There must be a generator in the basement or something, I said. By the way, Anna, are you trying to hurt me by doing that? Because if you are, you're doing a good job.

Mini, look in that box for Band-Aids, Anna said, ignoring me. But she held her makeshift rag a fraction lighter against my head. Part of the silky fabric escaped and covered my face.

Jesus, how bloody big are these! I said, my voice muffled under the silk. Magellan's sail was smaller than these undies!

Both girls were giggling now. I heard the peeling of Band-Aids and moments later my vision was free and Anna moved in close to stick them on, one hand applying and the other pinching the cut closed. Her mouth was open in concentration and her breath smelled like strawberry lip gloss.

Okay, she said, that should hold, but keep some pressure on it until the bleeding stops.

I took the underwear and held it up against my cut. I watched the reflections of Anna and me in the glass window, imagining a different version of us.

I looked cross-eyed at the underwear in my hand and said to Anna: Hang on, these aren't yours, are they?

Despite my injuries, she punched me in the shoulder, a real corker, and went and sat down on the floor, watching the doors at the front of the arcade.

Dave came back holding a big black torch. He was speechless for a moment when he saw me pressing frilly pink undies to my head.

They're Anna's, I said and laughed at my own joke.

All the phones in this place are out, he said. Power too. Cell-phone network, everything. There's no one here except a big old guy who worked at the nut shop – I think he must have had a heart attack.

Nuts, I said to fill the silence.

Dave looked at me like I'd just insulted his president, which I'd unintentionally done on the day we met. Really, I liked the guy – it was an accident.

Sorry, I said. My grin didn't help the situation. Cracking jokes was my default. Then I remembered the people who'd chased us and Mr Lawson's hollow stare, like he wasn't all there, and my grin faded.

Okay, I said. We have to find help. There must be people somewhere, emergency crews on their way here or something. Right?

Dave shook his head.

What? Anna asked.

They would have been here by now, he said. Think about it. Our subway was hit nearly an hour ago. All that shit and destruction out there – nothing in New York takes this long for cops and fire-fighters to respond. Something like this, there'd be helicopters buzzing overhead and a million sirens all around us by now.

I realised he was right. Almost every block in Manhattan had a police car permanently parked on it for rapid response. Hell, Grand Central Station had about a hundred armed National Guards all around it—

Why don't we head for Grand Central? I said. There were all those army dudes there this morning.

That was because the President was coming to town today, Dave explained. They've been there all week, extra cops too.

So why don't we go there? Anna said, getting to her feet. It can't be too far from here. Then we're closer to the UN building.

Dave looked towards the glass entry doors and nodded.

We're on 43rd Street here, he said. We go out that door and turn right, cross over Fifth and Madison and we're there, Grand Central.

How long will that take? Mini asked, shivering with cold and wringing out her scarf. The water pooled with what was already puddled around our feet.

If we run, five minutes, Dave said. Walk, ten.

We run, Anna said.

I nodded and could see the girls seemed relieved. We zipped our parkas up to our necks and I tossed the bloodied underwear into a bin. Anna, the only one with a backpack since the subway, put the medical box inside and tightened the straps around her shoulders.

Want me to take that? she asked Dave, holding out her hand for the torch.

He shook his head and gripped it in his fist. It made me feel better to see him holding it that tightly, his knuckles tense.

Wait a sec, Mini said, as we stood looking towards the doors. What if there's more of . . . *them* out there?

No one said anything.

They were . . . they were *drinking* from people, Mini went on. What the hell is wrong with them?

I glanced at the others. They looked as hesitant as I felt.

I don't know, Min, I said gently. But we can't stay here all day. We have to find where everyone's at.

But—

If we see any people we're not sure about, we run the other way, all right? I said, trying to look like I knew what I was talking about. Dave, we're two blocks away from Grand Central. Give us a back-up place.

Back-up place?

You know, some other place we can go, just in case, yeah?

I could almost hear the wheels turning in Dave's big head as he thought.

We could run into the library, he said. That's not far from Grand Central. Or we pick one of the tall buildings on Park Avenue, somewhere with a view.

I nodded and moved towards the arcade entrance. Dave and I each took an end of the bench seat and dragged it back just enough to get a door open.

I quickly motioned the others out. Dave led the way and we set off at a jog behind him, me at the rear.

I didn't want to think about what would happen if there weren't any police or soldiers at the station, but as we covered the next block and I saw the devastation around us, my heart sank. I had made up my mind before we'd even reached Grand Central: we had to find somewhere to hide.

3

This had to be terrorists, Anna said and none of us doubted it enough to argue with her now.

There were bodies outside Grand Central Station. Dead bodies lining the street in sickening fan-like patterns, as if they'd been blown out of the doors. Beyond the bodies was a massive crater spanning four lanes of road that seemed to be erupting with junk. Clumps of broken concrete and bitumen made walking almost impossible.

I looked up to where the Grand Hyatt used to loom over the station and saw that only a skeleton of the high-rise hotel remained. Just the *H* of the *Hyatt* sign was left and the windows had blown out, revealing the concrete slab floors, some barely hanging on to their metal reinforcing rods. Thousands of tonnes of glass and concrete were in the station, now a smoking shell without a roof. As I watched, a mattress slid from an open floor of the hotel twenty storeys up and fell like a leaf, seesawing earthwards until it was swallowed up in the wreckage below.

Mini and Anna moved closer to me as I turned to Dave and said: We need to find somewhere with a view. Somewhere we can see the extent of what's happened so we can plan where to go next.

He nodded and looked up and down the section of Park Avenue that split around Grand Central as though the train terminal was a big traffic island. The only place I could think of was the UN building.

Okay, he said, pointing north. We go left at the first corner and head up Madison to 49th, where we go west one block to 30 Rock.

30 Rock? I asked.

I vaguely remembered him talking about a group of us going to the Rock's viewing platform while we were in town.

Yeah, you know, 30 Rockefeller Plaza – the GE Building? That's where the Top of the Rock Observation deck is. Got 360-degree views up there, far as the eye can see.

Good, I said. Mini nodded in agreement, but I was worried about Anna – she was staring off into the distance. I tugged on her parka sleeve.

How far? she said absently.

She was transfixed on the bodies in the street. I knew part of her was getting further away from us every second we spent here. I itched to get moving.

Five minutes, Dave said. Come on, let's bounce.

We started moving at a jog, single file, same formation as before. Dave nearly stopped at a couple of crushed US soldiers. I'm not sure if they were National Guard or Marines; I don't think any of us would have known the difference – even Dave, whose dad had been an accountant for the US military in the Gulf War. Whoever these soldiers were, they'd done their job. What a job . . .

Madison Avenue's buildings seemed mostly fine. The rain had picked up again, but aside from the abandoned cars and one body in the street we didn't see anything. No one complained about the rain or slowed down to look at the body. I silently thanked Dave for not taking us anywhere near it.

I wondered when it was I'd started thinking a dead body on a city street wasn't worth investigating. Was this what it had been like for our soldiers in Iraq and

Afghanistan? Probably not. There, they were surrounded by people and wouldn't have known who was friend or foe, or who might have a bomb hidden under their clothes. I didn't know which would be worse – being in a country where you might get blown up at any second, or being here, with unknown freaks that chased you and . . . well, *drank* you. I thought about the pistol back in the subway carriage – should we have taken it?

We rounded the corner of Madison Avenue onto 49th Street. It looked at first like the type of scene I'd been daydreaming about. There were four fire engines, their blue and red lights flashing. Rows of steel pedestrian barriers lined one side of the street; enough to cordon off the entire block. But after a few seconds, I realised this scene wasn't quite my dream. There were no people. No policemen, no firemen, no survivors. Not even dead bodies.

I kept expecting to come across someone in uniform who'd say to us: *Get your butts down into the subway tunnels with the others*, or *What are you doing out here? Why aren't you waiting in the buildings with everyone else?* I knew from our orientation earlier in the week that New York was home to ten million people, give or take – over twenty if you counted the surrounding sprawl. And so far we'd seen evidence of maybe only a few hundred.

We rounded the first big engine, one of those trucks with the massive ladders that was driven from the back, and came up to a FDNY Emergency Response Vehicle – basically a bus decked out with equipment, a mobile fire-fighting-cum-command centre. The back doors were open, revealing more computers and comms gear than a space shuttle.

I'll check inside, Dave said and he bounded up the stairs of the bus.

Anna and Mini moved away from the trucks and took shelter under the entrance of 30 Rock, about twenty metres away.

Dave reappeared at the front of the bus and sat in the driver's seat, manning the radio. Between the sound of him switching frequencies and the rain, I'm not sure if I heard distant gunfire or not. All that came out over the radio speakers was static and sometimes a strange sound like a woodpecker, or that sound kids make when they're playing soldiers, and pretending to fire a machine gun.

There's nothin', Dave said, appearing next to me with a hand-held radio. He seemed a little deflated, down to my size.

There's nothin' on the radio . . .

All right, I said. We have to get to the top of the building and look.

I motioned *let's go* to the girls. Amidst the noise of the rain hitting the steel roofs of the fire engines, I heard Dave sigh.

Maybe just you or I should go up, he said. The girls will be slow. One of us should go and take a look and come back—

Dave, I said, turning to look him in the eye. Mate, whatever we do, we're gonna stick together, all right? This . . . this is weird shit. You saw Mr Lawson. You saw those people who chased us. We have to stick together, it's our best chance. Come on, brother, let's go.

He looked at the torch and radio in his massive hands. His eyes had a big, sad, puppy-dog look I'd not seen before.

Dave, how many floors up is the observation deck?

Seventy, I think, he said. It'll be getting dark by the time we get up and back.

I looked left and right along 49th. Beyond the steel barriers on the opposite side of the street was a Fox News office. Its massive tickers were blank – even the emergency lighting must have been out in that building. I checked my watch: almost 3 pm. It would be dark by 4.30 and Dave was right – it would take a long time to walk up seventy flights of stairs.

Look, it might be good to stay up there for the night anyway, I said. We stay up there, get warm and dry, and who knows, maybe in the morning we'll be able to see where everyone else is hiding.

Dave considered the idea. All right, he said, then walked towards the back doors of the FDNY bus.

What are you doing? I asked, as he shone his torch inside and started rummaging through some big plastic tubs.

There might be some useful stuff in here, he said, pulling out boxes of blankets and plastic sheeting and gas masks.

I went to the closest truck, opened the door and climbed into the cab. I checked out the front and back and found nothing useful except a big heavy FDNY jacket. I took it, figuring it was more substantial than what I was wearing.

When I stepped out of the truck I saw Dave was wearing a backpack with an axe handle poking out the top like an antenna. He tapped a large object by his feet – it looked like an engine and was about the size of a household microwave.

Generator, he said as I walked over to him. He put a gas bottle on top and I draped the FDNY coat over it. He used his left hand, I used my right, and together we picked up the generator by the metal piping that ran around its edge. I grunted as I stood. Dave smiled at me.

Come on, let's get this over with, I said as we made our way towards the entrance of 30 Rock. At least the rain was starting to ease.

As we headed towards the door, I noticed that Mini and Anna had wandered off and were now looking at something in the middle of Rockefeller Plaza. We left the generator by the entry and went over to join them. Above us, a forest of flags on poles flapped in the winter breeze.

The girls were gazing down at what had once been the ice-skating rink. By the time I was standing between them, I wished I was in the arcade again, only the one I'd dreamed of; the one with the nice lady and the hot drinks and the busy policemen . . . Before us, it looked like more than just a bomb had gone off. All that was left was a massive crater. The whole space that had been the skating rink was gone, reduced to a hole in the earth that steamed and hissed.

This is Rockefeller Plaza, Dave said, his voice as distant and unbelieving as his expression. I've skated in here . . .

I watched a tear roll down Anna's cheek. We'd toured Rockefeller Plaza on our first day in New York. I decided it was hardest when we saw something we recognised reduced to this – something we had directly experienced at some time, taken away with violence. The underground level of the plaza bore ominous cave-like mouths; jagged, black holes that I imagined went to the centre of the world. There were uniformed bodies everywhere. It was as if the earth had opened up here, swallowing the city and anyone who'd tried to stop it, those fine men in uniform who ran into harm's way.

Come on, I said. Let's go.

Mini put an arm around Anna's shoulder and pulled her in close, and we turned to head into 30 Rock.

A horn blazed, piercing the air. It seemed like the loudest, most foreign noise I'd ever heard. I looked but there was nothing, yet the sound grew louder and all of a sudden a car went flying along Fifth Avenue. In the view we had from 49th, it was gone in under a second, but we had all seen the same thing: the car, one person at the wheel and obviously leaning on the horn, several people on the hood and roof trying to get to the driver inside.

A few seconds later, a crowd of twenty or more people went running along in pursuit. The horn grew more distant until it faded to nothing. Nothing but deathly silence.

Minutes passed before any of us moved. Mini was the first to turn around and make for the entrance to 30 Rock. We followed her in shock. At the entrance I took a deep breath, preparing to pick up the generator again, when I heard another noise. A jet aircraft – low, fast, ripping through the grey sky somewhere above us. We all craned our necks and looked, but it was gone as quickly as it had come. No use shouting at it to come back. It seemed to be heading northeast but I wasn't sure.

We heard a deafening boom that could have torn a hole in the sky, and it echoed around us in surround-sound as we pushed open the doors. The slush at our feet was left behind as we entered our new home. It was cold and hard and dry and quiet, and I loved every bit of it then and there.

This was 30 Rock.

4

Dave was right. The main observation deck was seventy floors up.

What can I say, Dave? I told him. When you're right, you're right.

Wow, Dave was right? Mini said.

He grunted and passed over a water bottle he'd pulled from his FDNY backpack.

The lobby said the Top of the Rock is on floors sixty-seven to seventy, Anna said.

Great, I said, catching my breath and rubbing the soreness out of my arms.

We were sitting on the fire stairs at the 21st floor. The emergency lighting was on, so at least we could see where we were going. I made the mistake of looking up the void between the handrails: if there were a stairway to heaven, this could have been it. It was a depressing distance to travel with baggage.

Anna had my FDNY jacket stuffed into her backpack, and she and Mini carried the twenty-litre gas bottle between them. My arms ached as if I was carrying everything myself; carrying it all and then some.

Okay, this is messed up, Mini said. I'm sick of carrying this friggin' piece of shit up all these stairs.

I loved it when Mini swore. She was from Taiwan, yet she knew more English swear words and used them more frequently than anyone I'd ever met. Earlier in the week, when we'd formed into our little groups on our second night at the hotel, she'd taken a bottle of vodka from the mini-bar and got drunker on that tiny bottle than I'd seen my uncle after he'd sunk a whole case of beer. We'd called her Mini after that. It was also short for her name, Min Pei, and it suited her.

Can't we leave it here? Anna said, rubbing her arm. I can't carry it anymore.

Dave went to the generator and unscrewed the cap on top. He dipped his finger in and sniffed at it.

This is gassed up already, he said. He pulled out his torch and starting reading from the side of the generator: Evopower generator . . . blah blah . . . Here we go – three sockets, nine-litre capacity, nine-hour running time.

He flicked the torch off and turned to me, his eyebrows raised.

What? Does that mean it uses a litre per hour?

Doesn't say, he replied. Let's just assume it does, as a worst case.

Okay, that will be enough to run for a few hours tonight if we want, I said. And a few hours tomorrow if we need it. We'll leave the gas bottles here.

I got to my feet and readied to move on.

You don't think we *should* leave it here though, do you? Anna said as she stood up. She narrowed her eyes at me and I saw her use an expression I'd not seen before – ugly.

You think we might be up there for a while, don't you? she pressed. I could no longer smell her strawberry lip gloss, even though she was standing close to me.

You think this is it? she said. You think we've gone from being stranded in the street to being stuck at the top of a skyscraper? That's insane! What if there are people in this building like the ones we saw in the street? What then, boy genius? Wait for them to come and eat us? You're crazy!

Funny, I was starting to think the same about her.

Before anyone could speak I got my vindication – the lights in the stairwell flickered. They remained on, flickered again, and then there was that distant, demolition noise I'd heard when we'd first emerged from the subway. Actually, we felt it more than heard it this time.

What was . . . ?

That was a building falling down, Anna, I said.

Oh my god!

Her eyes were as wide as saucers. She gripped the handrail and looked down the stairwell to the ground, twenty-one floors below.

Oh my god . . .

It wasn't *this* building, Dave said, and his deep voice seemed to calm her. She looked up at him and nodded.

Come on, I said, you guys have carried that gas bottle as high as you can. If you can't carry it anymore, set it down and I'll come back for it later.

I motioned to Dave. He picked up his side of the generator and we set off climbing again. It was so damned heavy I started to wonder if Dave was carrying his share of the weight.

We stopped again at the 50th floor, just long enough to have a drink of water and sit down for a bit, and then we were off.

At the 65th floor Mini starting gasping for air and looked like she might faint. Anna and I sat her down and fanned her, while Dave tried the fire door. He used the generator to jam it open, then came back and we all half-carried Mini through it.

The room beyond was a big, expansive restaurant, complete with floor-to-ceiling windows and a good hundred or so tables arranged around a dance floor.

The Rainbow Room, Dave said. My dad took my mom here once.

The new surroundings seemed to perk Mini up, and before long she was walking around on her own, exploring.

Anna perked up too. She wandered through the place, calling *Hello!* every minute or so. Dave disappeared into the kitchens, and Mini helped herself to a Coke from behind a massive bar.

I went to a window and saw we were up amongst the clouds. All around us were marshmallows in various shades of grey, cocooning us in, but also blocking the view. I was disappointed; I'd looked forward to proving to the others that coming up here was a good move, the right think to do. I was hoping we'd be able to look out at the sprawl of Manhattan and pick out places where other survivors might have congregated. Still, at least we were warm and safe. And I was glad we'd put some distance between us and the city streets before night fell.

I heard doors bang open and turned to see Dave emerge from the kitchen, steering a big waiter's trolley across the dance floor towards me. His grin was almost as big as the steel buckets he'd stacked up.

Freezers were out but they're still cold, he said.

He pulled the cart up to a table at the window where Mini sat drinking her Coke.

I found ice-creams of every flavour imaginable. We've got a dozen different kinds of chocolate alone!

All right! I said, and took a seat opposite Mini, who'd finally cracked a smile. We lined up the buckets of ice-cream in the centre of the table and used the heavy cutlery that had been set out for dinner service. Anna arrived and added a bowl of fruit salad to the table, but we made so many jokes about it that in the end even she didn't eat any.

We'll figure this out, I said, running a finger down the steel side of the ice-cream bucket as it sweated onto the linen tablecloth.

Where would everyone have gone? Anna asked. From here, I mean.

Home.

I nodded, thinking about the way Dave had said that word. Confidently, as if that's all there was to say about it. But I guessed he was right. If you worked in this building and saw the city had come under attack, through bombs or missiles or whatever, then as soon as you thought it was safe you'd head home. You'd run through the streets and over bridges and through the rain and dust and ash – you'd stop at nothing to be with your friends and family. I would, Dave would, anyone would. You'd go to your loved ones. I could imagine the news footage that would run for days and weeks afterwards, showing a million examples of mass evacuations from Manhattan office buildings.

The room was getting darker now. Mini rummaged through Dave's backpack and produced a lighter, then lit the two candles on our table. Dave leaned back to light another two behind us. The room felt warmer with that orange glow on our faces.

Tomorrow, when the clouds clear, like maybe early in the morning, I said – and Dave nodded that he agreed – we'll be able to look around us.

There's binoculars and stuff on the observation deck, Dave said. We'll be able to see everything from there. It's an awesome view, awesome . . .

ALONE

Anna and Mini were silent and we sat at that table and kept eating ice-cream until night came. It was better here, I told myself, better for all of us.

5

The night was pitch black. We curled up on couches in the lounge area and I watched a lit-up red exit sign by the door. I wanted to get to sleep before it blinked out. At one point I realised that of all the things to worry about, I was obsessing over how long the emergency lighting would stay on in the building.

What if we end up like . . . *them*? Mini said.

We won't, Dave answered quickly, like he'd been thinking the exact same thing at that moment.

How do you know? We don't even know what's wrong with them!

There was silence and then a muffled sound, as if someone was crying and trying to hide it.

Look, there's nothing we can do tonight, I said gently. Nothing until we see what's happened. Till we see where everyone's at, when the sun's up. There'll be more answers in the morning.

My eyes closed and I fell asleep for what felt like seconds but could have been hours.

I can't wait until morning, Mini whispered into the darkness.

Sleep, Min . . . It'll come quicker that way.

If only it were that easy. Maybe it was, I thought. Maybe sleep would change everything.

When I woke, it was light. Anna and Dave were already up, their faces pressed against the glass like any other tourists. Then I remembered that Dave wasn't a tourist; he was looking intently at a view he probably knew as well as I knew Melbourne's skyline. Mini was still asleep on her couch, a few paces from my own. All I could see of her was her red and black spiky hair, which peeked out from the layers of white table linen she'd used for blankets.

I got up before remembering that I'd stripped down to my underwear in the night. My clothes were hanging over the backs of dining chairs and still looked damp but I shrugged them on anyway.

I stood there in my cold jeans and T-shirt with the FDNY jacket pulled tight around me and looked out at the view before us. There was an early morning mist rolling in from the east and blanketing parts of the city, but the visibility was enough to cause a heavy weight to settle in my stomach. It was as if the city had been designed by Jackson Pollock. My dad has lots of his prints around our house and to me his artwork represents chaos. And that's what the mess of Manhattan looked like, minus the vivid colours. It was unbelievable.

We should go up to the observation deck, Dave said. We can check out the city with binoculars. Watch it as the day clears.

I checked my watch; it was almost 9 am. Anna went over to wake Mini and I moved in beside Dave. He looked at me with anger, but I knew he wasn't mad at me. I could sense what he was thinking. Our view was to the west; his family lived in Brooklyn, to the east. He'd be able to see in that direction when we got up to the observation deck.

Come on, mate, I said.

I motioned for him to lead the way upstairs, which he did without speaking.

The observation deck on the 67th floor was indoors, and like the Rainbow Room it was deserted. The four of us moved as one and the first direction we looked was east.

Still can't see much on the other side of the East River, Dave said. He sounded almost happy, as if there was good news headed his way once the sky cleared.

He ended up staying there for a while, a lone sentinel looking in the direction of home, and we gave him space. As the sun rose higher in the sky and the view cleared, his mood shifted and ours shifted with it.

Manhattan was in bad shape. It was hard to get an exact picture of the destruction, because we couldn't see much detail with the naked eye and the binoculars only allowed you to focus on one place at a time. I'd zoom in on a building that was half collapsed into a street, but miss the buildings flattened all around it. The small glimpses between buildings revealed streets that looked cluttered or barren. I realised that we'd need to be higher up, in a helicopter or something, to understand the true extent of the catastrophe. Unless this was worse than just Manhattan . . . But I didn't want to think about that.

I pointed my binoculars south and saw the Empire State Building was still standing, as was the Chrysler. From here, I couldn't tell if any other landmark buildings had come down, but I knew some must have. There were plumes of smoke rising from several spots around the city, particularly to the south in Lower Manhattan.

The sky there was dark and ominous compared to the steam that drifted up into the sky closer to us.

After a while I gave up on the magnified view and left the south platform. Even though it was protected by big sheets of glass, I'd felt a little queasy about going near the edge. I went inside, sat down, and settled for watching the view to the north. Dave came over and joined me.

The Williamsburg Bridge is the only one that seems to be standing, he said. It's piled up with cars and stuff, but I think we'd still be able to walk across it. I can't see all of it from here though.

I nodded absently while gazing out at Central Park and the neighbourhoods that surrounded it. Together they looked like a large-scale courtyard garden. The Hudson River seemed calm as it disappeared out of sight to the west. Up here, everything seemed calmer.

There are smaller bridges further up the East River too, at Second and Third Avenues, 145th, and a few others.

They're still standing?

Can't see them from here. Can't see much of the 59th Street or RFK-Triborough Bridges either, but it looks like there's smoke comin' from Roosevelt Island.

There's plenty we can't see at street level from up here. Plenty.

We sat in silence for a moment. I think Dave liked the fact that a lot was still unknown; in a way, that was one of the only things keeping him together. I was glad he was so optimistic. If he started to lose it, the rest of us would too.

What was that bridge up there? I asked, pointing to the spot where a bridge had spanned the Hudson. The stubby ends of the suspension bridge were all that remained, just a beginning and an end but no middle.

George Washington, he said flatly.

A small explosion mushroomed up to the east of Central Park and we watched as a multi-storey apartment building fell to the ground like a house of cards. From our vantage point it looked tiny, but I knew it must have been at least twenty storeys. Dave and I shared a look before turning back to the window. There was now only a plume of dust and smoke where the building had been, and the wind carried it slowly across the park.

Might have been the gas main, I said, watching the wisps of destruction suspended in the breeze.

Could have been anything, Dave said. A tanker going up, or an unexploded bomb or missile just going off now.

I realised there were no aircraft visible – none of the commercial traffic I'd constantly seen over this skyline all week and no fighter jets either. But there were some slipstreams in the sky, at least a dozen of them between the clouds. Someone was up there.

This was an attack, wasn't it? I said. I mean, this was a *country* attacking the US, something big, something planned, beyond what terrorists could do. Like you said, bombs or missiles – someone smashed this city and made its people . . . I mean, those people who chased us, they weren't normal . . . They were infected by, with, something . . .

Yeah, Dave said, looking sombre. Something like that.

Do you think we'll end up like them?

Dave shook his head. If it was going to happen it would have happened already, he said. Whatever it was probably got washed away by the rain.

I heard footsteps behind us and then Mini and Anna appeared. They'd been up on the outdoor deck of the 70th floor. The expressions on their faces seemed frozen – they both had that punch-drunk look we'd all shared when we emerged from the subway and saw this new world for the first time.

Should we go and look around this building a bit? See what's below us? I suggested, wanting to keep everyone busy.

Mini nodded but Anna looked out over my head at Central Park.

Come on, Dave said. Let's go and eat. Then we'll look around.

Anna shook her head, news in her eyes.

The mist cleared while we were up there, she said. We can see some spots where Manhattan meets the River – New York Harbour or whatever, to the south, the southwest . . .

And?

Anna looked at Mini who sat stone still on the seat. We know where all the people have gone, she said.

Before she could say anything else, Dave and I raced up to the 360-degree viewing platform on the 70th floor and hurried to check out the areas where the city met the water . . .

There were thousands, tens of thousands of people, massed by the shorelines. They weren't trying to escape the island of Manhattan and didn't appear to be talking to one another. They had the same vacant look as the people we'd seen yesterday. It was clear these people were after only one thing: a drink. They clamoured for places by the Hudson and drank, and their thirst seemed insatiable. But it didn't appear like they were fighting over the water or for a good position – they were sort of . . . grazing, like cows and horses do on grass. It was as if they had to keep their mouths wet at all times.

Dave pointed to something and I angled the big fixed binoculars in that direction. As soon as they focused, I gasped in spite of myself. There, a few blocks south of our position, in a deserted section of Fifth Avenue, was a group of around fifty people. Some of the group were picking up the slush from the street and eating it like you'd eat a snow cone or a Slurpy from 7-Eleven. But it was the ones crouched over human forms that made me shudder.

As I zoomed in on the face of one, he suddenly looked up in my direction as if he sensed my presence. There's no way he could have seen me from the street, but I swear his eyes locked on mine for a second. I knew I would dream about that face, that it would be in my nightmares. He had blood dribbling down his chin and dark red lips, and when he turned his attention back to the lifeless body lying on the road before him I willed him to drink from the gutter instead, but he bent down and drank some more.

6

We barricaded the doors to the Rainbow Room that afternoon. Holed ourselves up. All the time we worked I had that man's face in my mind. I worked until I could hardly lift my arms.

When we got back from the observation decks, Dave had suggested we use furniture to blockade the main fire stairwell, and it seemed a damned good idea to do anything to keep the people on the street from getting up here. We gathered restaurant chairs and tables and stacked them together in an awkward mass, then tied them with kitchen twine and anchored them to the balustrades and handrails, leaving a small tunnel so we could still get out. As a finishing touch we scattered a blanket of light bulbs on the landing behind it, a miniature glass minefield. The theory was that we'd hear anyone trying to make their way to the door. The light-bulb idea came from Mini and we all thought it was great. After a while she confessed she stole it from one of the 'Home Alone' movies, where the main character scatters light bulbs on the lounge-room floor to catch out some thieves. Genius.

As well as the main exit, there were two smaller fire escapes on this floor and we managed to screw those doors shut using a cordless drill from the restaurant's maintenance room. I'm not sure the building would have lived up to New York's infamous fire codes anymore, but after three hours' work we all felt better.

I still had the tool-belt on, so I paraded around a bit for the girls, swinging the FDNY jacket around my head and tossing it aside. They laughed and even Dave cracked up, I think more at my lack of muscles than anything, but at least the mood lifted.

Then Dave decided we should have a meeting. We sat at the same table as the night before – I'm not sure why we gravitated to that table again but we did – and drank juice and ate runny ice-cream and gourmet cakes. I found a pad and pencil and designated myself meeting secretary, although at that point we were yet to talk about anything noteworthy.

Man, these cakes . . . Dave said for about the millionth time, after eating his way through another huge slice.

You're going to end up in a sugar coma, Anna warned him.

I think we all are, I said and grinned a chocolate mousse smile at her.

The gas stoves are still working, Dave said. We should cook up some real food for dinner.

Dinner? Anna asked. Shouldn't we go to where . . . to where everyone else is?

Where's that?

There must be refuges, shelters . . .

Yeah, but until we know exactly where they are, let's stay where it's safe, Dave said.

He's right, I added.

Anna didn't reply.

Anyway, by real food I mean meat, Dave said. We should cook the meat while it's still good. There are coolers full of the stuff out there.

I'm a vegetarian, Anna said.

Of course you are, Dave said. I would be too if I was a Brit, with all that mad cow and stuff you guys have had.

I just don't believe in cruelty to animals, Anna replied. I don't believe in violence of any kind; that's why I came on this camp.

I was going to say my one lame vegetarian joke: *What, you don't hear carrots scream when you bite them?* but the moment had passed. Instead, I looked out the window at a city that was darkening by the minute.

Why had I come to this camp? Because my school wanted me to? For adventure? Because I wanted to get out of boring class-work back home, because I'd always done what others expected of me, because I'd seen violence too and wanted to make a difference somehow? Maybe it was to meet these people, my friends here. To meet Anna.

We should try to start the generator, I said. See if it works, maybe find a TV to run—

If the transmitters are down there won't be any stations, said Dave.

There might be satellite ones, I replied. Might be some news, maybe some non-US stations like the BBC. We should check the internet too.

Plenty of offices below us, Dave said. Bound to have TVs and stuff. Might be an emergency broadcast on or something, telling us what to do, where to go.

And what's going on, I added.

I scribbled down FIND TV, START GENERATOR and TRY INTERNET on our 'To Do' list, which already had the underlined words HOLE-UP/FORTIFY. No one else seemed interested in these notes; it was as if I was having a conversation with myself on paper.

And we could watch some DVDs, Mini said.

DVDs, I said, as I added it to the list. You're a genius, Min.

Sure, and I'll just go down to Blockbuster so we can have a movie night, Anna said.

I could see she regretted her tone when she realised Mini was hurt.

Sorry. It's a good idea, Min. It'll get our minds off stuff.

We have to accept we may be here a while, Dave said.

What's a while? Mini asked.

Day or two, maybe, he answered. It might take a while for help to arrive – if it's hard to get out of Manhattan at the moment, it must be just as hard to get in. It might take a while for help to come, you know?

We'll keep checking the view, take it in shifts, I said. Look around from the observation decks until we see something. Night-time too – we might see lights on in other buildings, might see some streets or neighbourhoods that have power. Once we find out where the other survivors are, we can move.

Why should we stay here at all? Anna asked. I mean, tonight, yeah, but if we think this may take a while to get fixed, why don't we go somewhere safer?

Safer?

Yeah, like a bank, or a police station, Anna said. Then if we're attacked by . . . by someone, we could hide in the vault or something.

We'd have weapons if we went to a police station, Dave said. Who knows, maybe the police and fire stations are refuges, full of cops and people like us.

And what if they're not? I argued. What if they're empty, like here—

What if this building's *not* empty? Anna said.

If there's anyone in this building, they'd be up here like us, Dave said.

Anna didn't look convinced.

But we could go to the UN building or—

And what if we get there only to find that we're locked out, and then we're stranded down there in the streets . . . with *them*, I said. I took a deep breath before continuing. Look – we go down there, there's risk. What if we become like them, like all those milling about the water, like Mr Lawson? Up here, there are three fire escapes we can use if we have to get out in a hurry. If we *did* set up in a bank or something, it would be too easy to get cornered – places like that are as hard to get out of as they are to get in. At least here we can see. We've got good views. We've got options. We can see if a rescue is coming, and . . . and we can see *them*. I feel safer from them, those . . . infected people, up here.

The others were silent, taking it in.

We should have a name for them, Anna said. The Sick, or the Infected? Something. Something to differentiate them from the real people we see – I mean, the normal survivors like us.

The Thirsty? Dave suggested.

The Thirsty? Anna said sarcastically. Like, look out Dave – there's a thirsty behind you?

The Arseholes, Mini said. The Scary Arseholes.

That works, I said with a grin. *Look out Dave – there's an arsehole behind you!*

The three of them laughed and Dave actually took a quick glance behind him.

How about the Chasers? I said.

Dave nodded approvingly.

Think about it, I said. They chased us, and they ran down those three guys we saw.

Why? Anna said. Have we thought about that? I mean, they're obviously sick, but why are they chasing people? Maybe we should try talking to one, going down there and approaching one.

Maybe, I said.

Maybe? Dave said in disbelief. If I had a gun in each hand and we approached just one of them – yeah, maybe then. But I'm not going down there on the streets. I've seen what some of them are doing. You've seen it too.

Why are they doing this? Mini asked.

She seemed younger and more innocent than the rest of us; it made me want to protect her.

Who knows? Dave said. We know they're thirsty and they're chasing after survivors.

Maybe it's anthrax, suggested Anna.

We all looked at her blankly.

Whatever has infected them, she explained. Made them Chasers.

Anthrax doesn't make you deranged like that.

How do you know what it does? Maybe it's a new strain that makes people evil.

Evil? I asked.

Yeah.

Like, what – we're good and they're evil?

You got it, Jesse, Dave said. Us and them.

I don't think it's that simple.

Evil does exist, Anna said. I know it.

I don't think they're evil, I said. They've just got a disease that makes them thirsty. They don't seem malicious – they just take whatever liquid is on offer, simple as that.

You really think so?

Maybe . . .

But they'd take us.

We're not on offer, Min, I said. They're not all bad.

We've seen them chase after living people.

Yeah, but maybe it's only the wounded they chase, I said. Like, people who have cuts and are bleeding.

Or maybe the Chasers who run after people were different to begin with? Mini said. Violent criminals or something?

We were quiet and I didn't know what to say, but I knew I had to fill the silence or I'd be thinking about this conversation all day.

Look, this infection could have been anything, I said. We know it's not in the air or we would have been infected by now.

Then how did the Chasers get infected?

Maybe it was in the air to start with, I said. Maybe Chasers are the people who were outside when the virus was dumped on the city. Then it cleared in the rain or something. I don't know . . .

Maybe they'll all drown down at the river, Mini said.

They're not drinking much, I replied. They're just kind of . . . sipping all the time, like they have an unquenchable thirst or dry mouth. My uncle lost all his saliva once, for like a month or something, and the docs never knew what brought it on or why his saliva came back.

What could cause that?

I don't know, I replied. Maybe it was stress or drinking too much, or being overweight.

Perhaps it was a small stroke or something?

Maybe.

Yeah, well maybe they'll get better then, Mini said. Maybe it'll wear off . . .

We'll have to wait and see, won't we? Dave said. Sooner or later, those Chasers will realise that they can't survive by drinking from the Hudson. It's tidal and salinated all along Manhattan island, I'm pretty sure. Once they figure that out, they'll probably head to the ponds in Central Park.

Will it kill them?

Salt water? If they're stupid enough to drink it for days on end, yeah, it'll kill them, Dave said. If they're stupid.

They're not stupid, Mini said. They seem like us, only sick.

They *were* like us, Dave said. And who knows, maybe this will wear off soon, like it did with Jesse's uncle, or the government will come with some kind of antidote for it. Until then, we should stay away from areas with obviously available water.

I nodded and noticed Mini wiping tears from her eyes. I knew she'd made other friends on the UN camp; maybe she was thinking about them. Or maybe she was just missing everything back home, like me.

Don't worry, Min, I said. This is America. They've got plans for everything here. Whatever this attack and outbreak is, there are smart people gathered somewhere right now trying to work out how to deal with it. Things are happening. For the moment it might seem like it's just us, but we'll stick together until help comes, okay?

She nodded. Anna didn't look impressed or convinced. A distant hollow-sounding rumble announced that another building was coming down. None of us commented on it. Something else lost forever.

What if it's not just here? Anna asked. New York, I mean. What if this is nation-wide and no one's coming to rescue us? What if America's gone – if everyone out there is like *them*, the Chasers? What if the only help we're going to get is in this room?

Anna's tone had a hard edge and I didn't like what she was saying. I didn't believe the people in this room were it. There had to be others out there, talking with their friends like me, or alone, or maybe even just going about their lives as usual.

This is a big country, Dave said. But you've got a point, Anna. There may have been attacks on other cities too. Maybe it's not just New York, maybe there are other places in the US that are as screwed as we are. But whoever did this, whatever this is, it isn't everywhere, I know it. There's no country on earth with the ability to strike against *every* American city—

How do you know? Anna was leaning forwards on her chair, her faced flushed. How!

Dave was going to fire back, but he got up from the table instead and stormed off into the kitchen.

Anna was silent at first, but after a while she seemed to cool down. I didn't care about the fight; at least it made Mini focus on the three of us rather than what was happening outside.

His family are out there somewhere, Anna, I said softly. His family are probably gone. We're not from around here; he's feeling this harder—

I know, Anna said, and she wiped away a tear and got up and went into the kitchen to be with Dave.

I felt a pang of envy then, in spite of everything. I started wishing that Anna and I had had the fight and it was me she needed to make up with. It was stupid thinking that way after all we'd been through, but I couldn't help it.

I'd felt like this before, when my dad told me he was getting remarried. We'd been fishing together one weekend at the Snowy River. Dad had given up his job in architecture to work as an artist for a bit and it was just him and me. But all that changed when he married Barbara – he went back to his office job and we moved to a bigger house. I've felt alone since then.

Come on, Mini, I said, leaning over and lighting the candles on the table. Let's see if we can work out the generator.

As I stood I turned to see what the others were doing. Dave was looking down and Anna was talking to him with her hand on his arm. They were together in that moment and I knew I had to let them be.

7

That night we used the generator for the first time. We ran it for a few minutes then quickly realised we needed to put it somewhere isolated, as the exhaust fumes were pretty disgusting. We set it up in a separate bar section of the Rainbow Room and shut the double doors, trailing extension leads out to our common area.

We ate well at dinner, cooking up big servings of food, even though we weren't sure whether the gas was on for good or if we were just using what was left in the pipes. Dave climbed under the stoves and shut off the gas to all but one, in case the pilot lights were using up whatever precious little gas remained in the system. I noticed we were starting to make more of these types of measures, as if we expected to be here for a while.

As darkness fell, we retreated to our couches. I leaned against a pile of cushions and listened to my friends talk. Their chattering had a reassuring metre to it; a background track of hope as I slowly fell asleep. In spite of everything I felt lucky. As annoying as Dave could be and as ugly as Anna sometimes was and as fragile as Mini was becoming, at least they were here with me. We were all in this together.

Sometime during the night the emergency lighting went out. We couldn't pinpoint exactly when, because we were all asleep at the time. It wasn't until I got up to go to the toilet at around 4 am that I discovered there were no lights. Even the glowing red exit signs were out. It was the same with most of the city. It seemed like many of the surrounding buildings' emergency lights had either gone out completely or were flickering off and on, like a neon tube on its way out. It was as if a blanket of darkness had been thrown over the streetscape. I missed the glow of the exit signs, yearned for them in the dim pre-dawn; they'd been my Southern Cross, constant in the darkness. I sat by the window and thought about all I missed, until sunrise brought me back to our grim reality.

Over breakfast we speculated again about who could have done this. Mini was adamant it was China, and she got really flustered explaining to Dave that Taiwan is not a part of the People's Republic.

Maybe it was the CIA, Mini said.

Anna laughed at that and we all joined in.

I don't think we know enough to point the finger yet, she said.

But it *could* have been the CIA, for all we know, I said, causing Anna to laugh again. I got the feeling she was laughing *at* me, not with me.

Russia, Dave said. No doubt, one hundred percent indisputable fact, it was the Russians.

I guess the world's lucky you don't have your finger on the button then, Dave, I said. Nuclear response, much?

Go ahead, laugh, he said. My parents had to do nuclear-attack drills when they were at elementary school in case a launch from Russia was detected – they'd have to sit under their wooden desks in the brace position, like they tell you on a plane.

And I'm sure that position would be just as helpful in a nuclear attack as it would be at thirty thousand feet when a wing falls off, I said, and both Anna and Mini laughed.

Dave shook his head. Russia's the only country that has the gear to do something on this scale, he said. What with all the bombs and whatever chemical agent it was that made people turn into Chasers like that.

The French have a lot of weapons too, Anna said, and I think Mini silently agreed because I saw her expression change when Anna spoke.

We ate cake for lunch that day. We were slowly eating our way through the restaurant desserts, persuading ourselves that they were perishable so we might as well enjoy them rather than watch them rot. I can pinpoint the exact moment I decided never to eat chocolate cake again – it was when Mini vomited up a flourless mud cake. Thick, gooey, snotty stuff came out of her nose and mouth at the same time and painted the window by our favourite table. Dave vomited when he saw her vomit, a stream of gloop that covered the chair I'd hastily vacated. Afterwards he seemed shaken and smaller, more like me.

We had no problems with water shortages, so luckily we could clean up the mess. The normal taps had bubbled and drained out the previous day, but then Mini pointed out the fire sprinklers in the ceiling. We'd found the service cupboards and shut off the inlet valves to the fire extinguishing system, trapping hundreds of litres of water that ran through the pipes.

Dave and I volunteered to go and fill the buckets with the fire hose, which was in the restaurant's cloakroom. It was at least a two-person job; someone had to hold the massive hose while the other held the buckets. While we worked, Dave told me that his dad owned a block of flats in Queens and he would go there with him sometimes and watch him do repairs.

Your dad must be pretty smart, buying up property in New York, I said.

Dave shrugged.

The city was different when he was growing up. Especially over there. Gettin' all expensive these days; different kind of people.

I was about to tell Dave to watch it with the hose – I was getting soaked – when he launched into a tirade about the tenants in his dad's flats.

They've got my dad by the balls. They're locked in on some kind of rent control so he can't get them out, doesn't earn anything near what he should. Mom and Dad should be comfortable by now . . . hell, he's always getting called out to fix something, and half the time it's nothing they couldn't fix themselves. He's away from home all the time. Too late to change that though. They're probably getting a divorce soon anyway because of some guy called Leo.

Dave spat out the name, then dumped the hose down and looked at the floor.

Scary thing is maybe my dad prefers to spend time at that place, he said quietly. He walked away, head low, and disappeared up the stairs.

I found him later on an outside observation deck, looking east. I sat next to him and thought about my own parents. I never really knew why they'd got divorced and I wondered if there'd been a Leo involved there too. I doubted it. I was only four when Mum left, but my few memories before that were of a happy family.

We spent the afternoon searching through the five floors below us, anxiously checking each apartment and office for survivors. The first few times we opened or broke down a door, my heart raced at the thought of what was behind it, but the rooms beyond were always vacant. As our hope of finding anyone began to fade, we decided to empty the rooms of anything useful, stacking our findings neatly along the hallways. We did this quickly so we wouldn't have to look at the pictures of families on fridge doors and dressers as we raided their cupboards and tried on their clothes and tasted their food.

Food was everywhere. By the time we'd been through half the floors between us and level 60, we realised we wouldn't have to ration anything. It amazed me how much food people kept, more still how long it would last. Long-life milk would still be okay to drink twenty-four months from now. Most cans didn't have a best-before date, and we found everything in cans: fruit, meat, vegetables, beans, lentils, milk, sweetened condensed milk, even cheese.

The fresh food we liked we bagged and then later carried up to the roof, letting the snow and cold winter air keep it chilled. The garbage and stuff going rancid we launched off one side of the building. That was more fun than it should have been. I joked that a cabbage hurled from this height would build up enough terminal velocity to go through a car's roof. We laughed and decided to try it out, craning our necks to see what happened seventy storeys below.

We talked about checking out every level in the building, but ended up stopping at the 60th floor. We already had enough food and stuff to keep us occupied for ages and besides, we'd enough of other people's things.

•

Check it out, Mini said. Her hair was dishevelled and she was wearing clothes she'd found in one of the abandoned apartments, only she'd tailored them to make the previously conservative gear more cutting edge.

Nice look, Min, I said. Taylor Swift meets Amy Winehouse.

Anna was swanning around in a formal dress and fur coat; I didn't have the guts to ask her how that fit in with the vegetarian thing. Dave had changed into an American football jersey, headband and kevlar vest that he'd come across somewhere.

I tried on an Armani suit because I knew it would have been expensive but then realised I was swimming in it. I'd also found a Spiderman suit in an office boardroom. It was preserved behind glass and mounted on a wall so I figured it was probably an original from the movie. I'd felt a bit guilty about smashing the glass, but told myself I could always return the suit after I'd tried it on. It fit pretty well, so I showed it off to the others, parading around the Rainbow Room until Anna rolled her eyes at me and I took it off.

We had found a massive plasma TV and DVD player in what looked like a TV studio, with props and lots of American football gear, and we set them up on the stage at the end of the restaurant. We'd also dragged mattresses up the stairs. I chose a queen size and arranged it on the restaurant's dance floor. Mini was just beyond my feet on a single mattress, and Anna was way off to our right on the carpeted area with two single mattresses stacked one on top of the other. She'd also stacked a wall of paperback books around her as a screen. Dave was near the windows on a roll-away bed.

As the room got darker, I lay on my makeshift bed, staring at the ceiling and listening to Anna play *Clair de Lune* on the Rainbow Room's grand piano. It was so beautiful it had made me forget myself and the world. After a while I wandered over and stood behind her. She must have sensed me there because she stopped playing and turned around.

I could teach you, she said.

I don't think so . . .

It's not as hard as it looks; the start's pretty easy.

I'll just watch and listen, I said.

She nodded and slid over so I could join her on the piano stool. I sat there with her for a while, stealing glances at her dark eyes and long eyelashes as she played.

That evening we ate a box of donuts we'd found, of all places, in someone's wardrobe, and watched an episode of *Arrested Development*. We'd each brought up DVDs that we wanted to see and they seemed to fall into three neat groups: comedies; real-life stuff like documentaries and concerts; and a stack of post-apocalyptic and war movies. We talked about the last group at length because, apart from Anna, we'd seen almost all of them. We didn't put one on to watch, but we talked about the plots and tried to remember anything useful.

We should have a plan in case any Chasers get up here, Dave said.

Mini went pale. You think they'll come up?

It's just a precaution, Min, I said.

You guys don't need to worry, Dave said. I found a gun this afternoon, a Glock.

Where? I said.

Under some guy's bed.

Do you know how to use it?

Yeah, my uncle went to Iraq and he taught me how to shoot.

I wasn't sure I believed him. Who teaches a sixteen-year-old how to use a firearm?

I'll teach you guys if you like, Dave said. How to load it too. We should work out some strategies tomorrow, find a couple of positions to defend ourselves from. If any Chasers do make it up here we should stick together.

We started talking about the number of scary movies we'd all seen where the characters would have been fine if only they'd stuck together. I guess that's what you wanted in a movie – lots of drama and conflict and crap. In real life I wanted none of that.

We left the television on and I drifted off in front of its blue-green glow. I dreamed I woke up in the Rainbow Room and found myself alone, only to wake for real in a sweat and call out my father's name. Mini answered back sleepily and told me I'd be all right.

I got up and switched off the generator, lit a few candles, then sat back down and ate some M&Ms.

Generator will be out of gas tomorrow, Dave said. His voice wasn't any louder than normal, but he was lying on his bed and his words seemed to echo around the near-empty room. Maybe it was also *what* he'd said that caused the echo; when I thought about what it meant I felt like I was going to choke.

We'll go in the morning and get some more petrol, Anna said. After breakfast. All of us. Look around a bit.

No one replied, but it seemed like everyone silently agreed. We needed the generator to keep sane, to provide a sense of normalcy.

We should run it for just three hours a day, I said. One of us can search the TV channels.

And just watch static? Anna said.

That might change, I replied. Check phone lines and the internet and other people's mobiles too.

All the things you think will offer salvation, Anna said, but we'll probably be disappointed.

Have to try though, right? Dave said.

We're better off just watching the view out the windows, Anna said.

We can charge up a laptop and batteries for our torches, I said, ignoring Anna's comment. Running the generator for short bursts is a good idea.

And the iPods, Mini said. We can't forget to charge the iPods.

We'd found about thirty iPods and iPhones. Mini and I had made a game where we listened to people's playlists and then tried to imagine the person who'd created it.

You should take the gun, I called out to Dave. Tomorrow, when we go to get petrol.

Yeah, he said quickly, as if it was something he'd already decided on.

I'll take one too, I said, trying to sound casual.

I thought I heard Mini make a sound, but it was Dave who spoke:

You found a gun as well?

I was silent for a few seconds, thinking about how to reply.

Why didn't you say anything sooner? Dave asked. By the sound of his voice, I could tell that he'd rolled onto his side and was facing me in the dark.

I don't know, I said, which was a lie. I hadn't told them because I was in two minds about taking it and I knew Dave would want me to.

What is it? he asked me. Pistol?

Yeah, I replied. It's a Glock like yours, I think. I left it where I found it, in an office drawer on the 63rd floor.

I heard him grunt and then roll back over to his sleeping position, his back to us and his face to the windows. For a while I thought I might hear him get up and go downstairs to find the pistol but he didn't, and within an hour he was snoring. He sounded like a big animal and the noise never faltered. The previous night Dave's snoring had been accompanied by Anna talking to herself in her sleep. I'd tried to make sense of what she was saying – *baloo, mowgli* – but it was all gibberish to me.

I felt my bed move, so slightly that at first I thought I'd imagined it.

Why didn't you tell us earlier about the gun? Mini whispered into my ear. Her voice, even at a whisper, had a faint wheezy sound and I remembered her asthma. Why didn't you tell us? she asked again.

I don't know, I replied, and then I felt her get under the quilts beside me. I rolled over and saw the shine of her dark eyes.

I guess I didn't want it . . . Didn't want to take it, I said.

But you're going to.

Yeah.

Why?

I don't know. I know the reason I *didn't* want it, but things aren't so clear anymore.

Mini was silent for a moment, then whispered: Can I stay here for a bit?

Yeah, sure, I said.

We lay on our backs, staring up at the chandelier above my bed. It was made of thousands of crystals, and despite there being almost no light, every now and then one would flicker, sparkling momentarily like we were beneath our own Milky Way.

chasers

We'd been on our own for three days already and seen no sign of salvation and I couldn't help but wonder if maybe this was all that was left. The thought made me lonely and I cried for a while and I know Mini noticed but she didn't make a sound.

8

Dave had his backpack ready on his bed by the time I woke. Mini was still asleep, but Anna had wheeled out a trolley of hot porridge with tea and coffee for her and Dave, and juice for Mini and I. Her eyes were clear and bright and I wondered if I'd ever feel as well rested as she looked.

The day was sunny and the sky seemed bluer than it had been for the past few days. We could see clearly to the east, and I walked over to the window and watched the city with my orange juice under my nose. There were no surprises that I could see. No alarms and no surprises.

Stairway's clear, Dave said as he dumped himself down at the table and got stuck into breakfast. I walked over and sat opposite him. When I saw the sweat on his face

I realised he must have moved our barricade on the main stairs by himself while I was asleep. I felt bad for not waking sooner, but I was tired and my body ached.

I've thought about it, Dave said in between big mouthfuls, and I reckon we should carry a load of gas cans up. And some ropes – fire trucks will have them – as many as we can.

Ropes? Anna said.

We'll join them up and make 'em real long, tie them to something up here, then drop them down the elevator shaft to hoist stuff up. More gas – whatever. We can prop the elevator doors open downstairs.

Beats lugging it up the stairs, Anna said. That's a good idea, really good.

I still felt half asleep. Didn't these guys need sleep like me and Min?

What if the lift blocks the shaft? I asked. I mean, if the lifts are between us and the ground floor, which is fairly likely, they'll be like corks in a bottle. What if you can't get past them?

Dave and Anna looked at me like I'd conspired to ruin their plan.

We should still try it, Dave said. He motioned to a table near us and I saw the pistol I'd told him about last night.

I loaded it, he said. Couldn't find any bullets in that office, but it's the same calibre as mine. I'll show you how to work it before we go down.

I nodded and ate my porridge. Anna beamed at Dave. I noticed the look he gave her and wondered what else he'd been up to that morning.

I got up from the table, walked over to the pistol and picked it up. It was much heavier than I'd imagined; I doubted I'd be able to hold it in my outstretched arm for long. I pulled back the slide and looked into the little rectangular space from where the spent bullet casing would spit out when fired, and I saw there was nothing in the chamber.

You don't chamber a bullet until you're going to fire it, just in case, Dave said.

I know, I replied, annoyed.

There's no safety on yours, said Dave. It's a triple-stage trigger, so basically you chamber a round, point and shoot. It's got fifteen rounds in the mag.

I nodded and tucked the Glock in the back of my jeans, which I made a little tighter at the belt. I remembered that Dave's pistol held seventeen rounds.

Aren't you going to finish your breakfast? Anna asked me. Dave had eaten all of his.

I shook my head and pulled on my jacket and boots.

Let's get a start on this, I said. I went over to Mini and gently shook her awake. Min, we're gonna head downstairs soon. Have something to eat.

She grumbled something funny and rude in reply and I grinned. I loved how she was like a nocturnal creature, the type of person who could quite happily invert their body clock and sleep by day. Part of me understood the desire to be alert against the darkness and asleep when I knew my friends were there to watch over me.

Mini quickly ate some porridge while Dave had seconds and Anna sat at the table drinking her tea.

I got my backpack ready, and when the others were finished I led the way downstairs, my friends falling in step behind me.

The darkness of the enclosed stairwell conjured up frightening ideas of what might lurk in the shadows, but we all had torches and Dave held his Glock out in front of him. Several times we stopped, my heart beating hard in my chest as I listened for foreign sounds, each time thinking maybe we should head back. Each time we continued on. As scary as it was, it was also exciting to be doing something new. We talked about the possibility of seeing other survivors, and before I knew it we were in the empty lobby and I wasn't so afraid anymore.

We exited onto Rockefeller Plaza. The open expanse, devoid of people, made me feel as though I was standing in an empty cathedral. It had snowed the previous night and there was a good covering of powder that was just starting to turn to slush under the winter sun.

There are footprints in the street, Dave said.

I followed his gaze and saw a single track of prints along the centre of snow-covered 49th Street. Not much else had changed since we were here last. The fire engines were exactly as I remembered them. The cargo doors of the FDNY bus were still open, as Dave had left them, and we carried the nine remaining gas bottles into the lobby of 30 Rock. The girls decided to stay there with them while Dave and I did a last-minute check for anything useful. We walked up to the two police cars that were parked nose to nose across 49th.

Try starting that up, Dave said, pointing to one while he got into the other.

My car had its driver's window open and the seat was wet, so without sitting down I turned the key in the ignition. After a few seconds it started up with a loud roar.

All right! Dave said, coming over to me. The other one's battery is dead.

I smiled. Let's let it run for a couple minutes, I said, remembering the first time I'd ever driven a car. Dad had taken me out to a vacant lot in our ancient Ford, but I'd hit a fence post because I could hardly turn the old beast. Three years later Dad would still tell the story with a laugh: the only obstacle for miles and I'd hit it. Dave probably wouldn't have had any trouble turning a heavy steering wheel like that, but in a cop car like this I reckoned I'd be a better driver than him.

Hey, what about cruise ships? I said to Dave.

What about 'em? he asked. He was sitting in the police car as he scanned the radio bands.

We could go to one if we get sick of 30 Rock. It'd be easy to defend – we could just raise the gangplank and—

I stopped cold.

A man was walking down the street towards us, along Sixth Avenue. Behind him there was nothing – at least four blocks of desolate nothing until a massive pile of rubble. Beyond that, I could just see the tops of the trees in Central Park.

Dave! I whispered urgently.

He killed the engine and got out of the car, his hand reaching up under his parka.

The man continued to walk towards us. He was on the sidewalk and he walked in a straight line. I think he was looking at us, but I couldn't be sure – he was still about forty metres away. His clothes draped down like they were soaking wet and too big for him. As he got closer I realised he was gaunt, his eyes sunk back in his head, his skin pale.

Stop there! Dave commanded him. He lifted up the gun and pointed it at him. Stop!

The man continued to walk towards us in a straight line.

He's doesn't look right, Dave said to me out of the side of his mouth, and he shouted again: Stop there! Stop!

He wouldn't stop. He wouldn't stop for Dave and I didn't shout out and I don't know why.

Despite the gun pointed his way and Dave moving a couple of steps towards him, the guy kept walking.

He's a Chaser! I said, watching him as he passed our corner at 49th. He was now twenty paces away and had a wide-open, crazed look in his eyes as he came towards us.

Please stop! I willed him and motioned with my arms outstretched and my palms facing towards him in case he was deaf. I was standing next to Dave and he yelled again: Stop! Stop!

The last ten steps, the Chaser suddenly changed. If he'd appeared a weak, incapable man from a distance, that facade shattered when he neared us. His eyes become deranged, intent, hungry. He launched himself at us, running the last few steps—

The noise of the gun going off seemed too loud and it echoed around the empty streets of Midtown Manhattan. I realised that Dave had turned his head away at the last minute and fired at the guy blind. I saw the bullet hit the Chaser, saw him drop to the ground. Dave and I took a few steps closer and watched as he did the most desperate thing: he touched the wound in his stomach, then looked at the blood on his hand and licked it. He was silent and so were we, but he was helpless. Didn't we warn him? Didn't he hear us say stop? Didn't he see the gun? He touched the bullet wound again and brought his hand up to his mouth. He didn't seem to be in pain, but as we stood there a couple of feet away Dave aimed the gun and shot him three more times.

He was dead. I looked at the Chaser and at the gun still smoking in the breeze, then behind us, to where Mini and Anna were standing on the street. I realised they must have seen the whole thing, or at least the final act. I ran to the gutter and threw up, then slowly walked over to Dave and took the gun from my friend. We went back inside 30 Rock, and I knew nothing would ever be the same.

9

The next day Anna made us bacon and eggs for breakfast. We didn't need to notice Dave's changed appetite to know that he was different now. I wished I could take back what had happened, the same way I wished I could forget what those bullets had done and the splatter of blood on the road. We'd warned that guy, hadn't we? What other choice had there been?

Afterwards Dave had carried a gas bottle in each hand all the way up the stairs and he wouldn't stop for a break even though the rest of us did, and we were only carrying two bottles between the three of us. I could hardly move my arms later on. At dinner time I'd found Dave in the men's toilets sitting on the ground and he'd told me to beat it.

Now his plate of food sat untouched and he stared out the window. I looked at the girls; they were both watching Dave.

I'm gonna go down again, he said suddenly. Open the elevator shaft doors, check them out, see about tying the last gas cans to hoist up.

Anna shot me a worried look.

You should stay up here to do the lifting, I said. I'll go down and do it.

I wanna see if I can get across to my parents. Head east, try Williamsburg, or maybe a tunnel.

His voice was flat, as if he didn't really believe what he was saying.

I'll try the Queens Midtown tunnel first, he said. Take that cop car.

But we need you here with us, Anna said, putting a hand on his arm. Please stay here.

I wanted him to stay for a different reason. What if he *did* go out there and saw that his family were dead? What if he saw them infected?

Dave, please . . . Anna said.

He looked at her like he was seeing her for the first time. I knew what Anna had said was true, that we needed him here, but I also knew she probably wouldn't have said that about me. The three of them were like their own little group and I'd never really be part of it. Well, maybe they didn't need me, but I needed them.

She's right, I said to Dave. They need you here. You three should stay together.

What are you saying?

What I just said.

Why?

I'll do it, I said. I'll go. See if I can find a way clear to your parents. I can do this, for us.

They all looked at me, waiting for answers.

Dave, you're the only one who knows how to shoot, I explained. You should stay here, it makes total sense. I'll go out at first light tomorrow, tie off the rest of the gas bottles to hoist up the lift shaft – from whichever floor is clear – then I'll take the police car and check out if there's any way over the East River. I'll try to get across, then be back before sunset.

Jesse, you don't know—

I'll take a map and follow it, I said. I gave a deflated laugh. Come on, Anna's right – you're needed here, man. If I can see a way that's clear out there, we can venture further out next time, together. Besides, if there's one thing I can do, it's run fast. If I have to ditch the car, I'll hoof it. I'm the fastest one here. None of those

Chasers out there can catch me – none of you could either, if it came to it.

I was trying to convince myself as much as them. Anna was the first to nod in agreement. I was hurt that she'd done it so quickly.

It's a good idea, she said. Dave stays here. You leave at sunrise tomorrow and see what you can find out for us.

Dave was silent as he sipped his coffee. Anna poured herself more tea and then some for me, and for the first time Mini held out her cup. I sat there and watched the steam rise and tried not to think about too much.

I had the afternoon shift on the observation deck. As I sat looking out at the city through binoculars, trying to figure out a clear route for my trip the next day, I thought about what it would be like to be on my own down there. Up here, the height of the place, the fact that we had to use binoculars to see any detail below, made it seem like we were somehow removed from reality. It was a bit like a game, what we'd been doing and how we'd been living; a game that only got real when one of us pulled a trigger down there on the street.

I'd seen things in the past four days; things other people wouldn't believe. Buildings glittering in the dark and becoming dust. Dead bodies. People no longer in control of themselves. Deranged men with a bloodlust, driven by some kind of primal greed. I'd had nightmares and terrifying thoughts, but nothing had prepared me for that terrible moment. A trigger being pulled. A life taken. I closed my eyes and saw blood and realised I would never forget what it's like to hear a pistol being fired up close, for real. For keeps. Was that Chaser less than human? Did it matter? I'd flinched on the first shot, and the second, and the third, but the fourth – that last shot – I didn't flinch. I'd watched it enter that man and kill him and by then he didn't flinch either. Death didn't seem so remote anymore – I was surrounded by it.

Here, Mini said, breaking my thoughts. She sat next to me and put a massive shopping bag full of chocolates and lollies between us.

Thanks, Min, I said.

I peeled a Snickers bar and ate it in four bites. Tomorrow I'd go down there alone and find the way for us all to get out.

You'll be all right out there, Mini said.

It felt good to hear her say that; it had been a statement, not a question.

But you don't have to go, she said. She smiled and I saw she had false candy teeth in place.

I laughed and she did too and the teeth fell into her lap.

I know, I replied. It'll be cool, Min. Chances are, I'll find help – find where the other survivors are hiding. If not, I'll come running right back here – I mean, I'll come back either way.

She nodded. She believed me more than I believed myself. She handed me something I'd seen her use before – her asthma ventilator.

Can you get me one of these while you're out?

Yeah, sure, I said and took it from her. Have you run out already? I thought we found you a couple of replacements downstairs.

Yeah, we did, she replied. It's no big deal. Just, if you see any drugstores, can you look for that brand for me?

Yeah, of course, I said, standing up. I'll keep my eyes peeled.

Huh? she asked as she followed me to the stairs.

What? Oh, I said, and tried to explain: Eyes peeled . . . It means that I'll keep my eyes open. I'll look for a drugstore for you.

Oh, right.

But in Australia we call them chemists or pharmacies.

Yeah, we do too, but we also call them drugstores. Our country has a big American influence.

Yeah, we do too, I replied as we entered the restaurant. It's everywhere, the whole world.

What's the whole world? Dave asked. He was sitting at the table we'd set up with maps of Manhattan and the US east coast.

Americanised, I replied, throwing my jacket on my bed. The whole world's Americanised.

Don't complain – that might be all that's left of us, he said, but despite his words he seemed a bit brighter. Maybe he'd had some rest. Or maybe it was all part of the Big Dave show, the guy who's so tough and strong and righteous. An act that was starting to unravel.

My dad once told me that no two countries with a McDonald's have ever gone to war against each other. That's gotta mean somethin'.

Yeah sure, whatever, Dave, I said.

I hadn't been ready for his mood to be so normal again. I'd been thinking all day about what to say to him and couldn't get past, *What choice did you have?* But I was glad if he was starting to accept that for himself.

He took me through the map. As I watched, he highlighted various routes, marking up the spots that we knew were blocked off by debris and fallen buildings. We did that for about an hour and then I packed my backpack and laid out my clothes for an early start. By then Anna had made dinner and Mini helped her carry it out. It was grilled tandoori chicken legs with rice and flatbread, and I swear it was the best dinner I'd ever had in my life. In the candlelight I noticed Anna sneaking looks at me a few times while the others were talking, and I started to get even more nervous about leaving this place in the morning.

We played a couple of card games after dinner and then Mini put on Stevie Wonder's *Superstition* and pumped up the volume to full and we danced. When we'd finally exhausted ourselves, we went to bed and chatted – the kind of chat you have when you've got your friends over to stay, when you can talk and laugh all night about the stupidest things. I guess we were trying not to think about the next day.

Half an hour later, I was waiting for the symphony of Dave's snoring and Anna's sleep-talking to send me to sleep when Dave said:

We need to get a signal set up. Something up on the roof.

We could paint a sign, I suggested. Something that an aircraft would see if they were passing overhead.

There'll be paint in someone's apartment or in the maintenance room.

I was thinking more like a signal fire, Dave said. Something that would be visible at night.

It might burn through the roof, though, Anna said. It's too dangerous.

Not if we do it right. In a drum or something, put some bricks down, Dave said. We don't have to have it going all the time, we can just have it ready to light if we see or hear something.

He's right, I said. And we know the roof's tiled, probably on a concrete base. We could even check the building plans. We should try to find those, actually, to make sure we really know our way around.

Dave grumbled something about checking out the basement the following day.

What would we burn? Mini asked. Paper?

Furniture, Dave said. Soaked in a bit of gas. Books. Table linen. Whatever we can find that will go up big and smoke good.

But we need those things, Anna said, then corrected herself: We need the gas, the petrol. And . . . We can't burn books.

I could, I thought. I'd be willing to burn anything.

What about that apartment with the big fireplace? Mini added. It might have wood and stuff?

That was fake, I told her. It's gas operated. We can't keep a fire burning on the roof permanently, but Dave's right – we should get something set up ready to light at the first sign of a rescue opportunity. You guys are right too, though – we can't waste what we need to survive. The price we pay for staying up here is that we have to lug everything up. We can't carry loads of oil or petrol up seventy flights of stairs every other day. But I'll keep my eyes peeled for anything useful when I'm out tomorrow.

Mini laughed at the word *peeled*.

Maybe our generator could power the lift and we could do a big trip that way? Anna said.

No. The generator can only power three electric outlets at once, Dave said. That's three normal domestic power loads, not an elevator that weighs tonnes. Not to mention the fact that we'd need to do some serious rewiring to try and rig it up. Can't happen.

How about the *building's* generator then? Anna asked. Could we fuel that up for the lifts?

No, that'd be for emergency lighting only, Dave said. We'd need an electrician or engineer to do a re-route like that, then heaps of gas or diesel or whatever the emergency generator runs on. Won't be happening.

The silence sealed it.

But we need to set that signal up ASAP, I said. I can't believe we haven't done it yet. Not that we've seen any cavalry coming over the horizon.

Not that we've seen much of anything, I thought but didn't add. No convoys, no airlifts, no big groups of people other than the infected.

I'll look for paint tomorrow, Dave said. And fuel for the fire – I'll start going though the rest of the floors below us, every apartment and office; you never know what we'll find.

Wait, said Anna. What if we do see someone coming, like a plane or a helicopter, and we've only got seconds to act? We'd need a proper signal for that, flares or something. We can't just rely on a fire – if it's been raining or snowing it might not start.

You're right, I said. I'll look for flares when I'm out tomorrow, check the fire engines. There must be some in there somewhere, for accidents and stuff.

And I'll set up the fire ready to go on the roof, just in case, Dave said. Maybe an armchair with a big stack of linen on it. I'll pour some liquor over it and protect it from the weather with some plastic sheeting. Until we can set up something better.

I waited for Anna to say something but she just gave a slight smile and nodded. None of us would have believed a few days ago that ideas like this would make us happy.

Maybe it was Godzilla, Mini said out of the blue.

Dave laughed.

Or that big-arse thing from *Cloverfield*, I added.

Or *Independence Day*, Dave said. Some kind of alien shit.

Or maybe this is some new reality TV show that we're part of, Anna said, and it's all just a big movie set with hidden cameras and they'll surprise us at any moment.

We were all quiet for a bit.

It would be nice if we could find out this isn't real, Mini said. Fake, like that fireplace. I'd really like that.

10

Each block that runs north–south will take you about two minutes at a fast walk, Dave said. Take it by car as far as you can. First, you try here—

His big index finger tapped a section of the map lit up by my torch. The sun was just the faintest glow on the cloudy eastern horizon.

Queens Midtown tunnel, I said, tracing my own route there in my mind's eye. Got it.

It's about an hour by foot, give or take; I doubt you'll be going slow, will you? And if the streets are clear you might be able to drive most of the way. Check it out. If it's blocked, then head south, probably take Third Avenue; it's a few blocks in from the shoreline.

Most of the Chasers have left the shores, Anna said. They could be anywhere by now.

It was true. Each day since we'd been here, we'd seen fewer and fewer of them around the shorelines. A few remained there, looking sick and worse for wear as time passed, but most of them had moved to Central Park. If one got weak and dropped to the ground, the others tended to ignore him. But if they dropped to the ground and their heads opened up as they hit the footpath, it was like watching seagulls at the beach diving on a chip.

I don't think they'll come after me, I said slowly, realising something as I spoke. They're just opportunists.

Anna shot me a look. Don't be so blasé about it, she said. They're probably more dangerous than we give them credit for.

What about the subway tunnels? Mini said. Surely they would have held – some must be okay to get through?

Yeah, probably, Min, I said. But they're dark and scary and we've had so much snow and rain there's probably been flooding. I bet lots of Chasers have gathered in there. I'd rather not go anywhere near the tunnels.

I thought back to the subway and the moment my torch beam had landed on that gang member's face. I remembered his twitching before he died and how scared I'd been of the gang members before everything turned to hell.

Queens Midtown is still our best bet if it's passable, Dave said. It's not far from here. It's a tunnel – and I hear what you're sayin', Jesse – but it's much bigger than a subway line. If you get to the point where you can see daylight coming from the other side, we'll know it's passable, so just get yourself back here. Hell, who knows, you might get lucky and be able to drive all the way there. My ma's probably flipping burgers at a refuge and my dad'll be shoutin' at the National Guard to come on in and find his son.

I nodded. Even if it was just bravado, I liked that Dave was feeling upbeat and I wasn't going to ruin his mood.

I picked up the backpack I'd taken from an apartment downstairs and filled it with enough food and water for twenty-four hours. I also had a spare torch, and Dave had already packed my pistol. The remaining space was occupied by the big FDNY jacket I'd rolled up in case I got caught in a downpour. I had trainers on my feet; they were a size too big but were laced up tightly and had good grip. I wore trackpants under military-style cargo pants, and a T-shirt with a thermal vest and a hooded sweatshirt over the top for warmth. I looked like

I was headed off to sports practice, albeit in a desolate city with a temperature of four degrees Celsius and an unknown number of people who were likely to chase after me for what was in my veins.

I'll be fine, I said, pulling the straps of the backpack tightly around my body. This'll be a walk in the park. Who knows, maybe I'll find a Porsche convertible and drive down Third Avenue with the wind in my hair and a beautiful babe in the seat next to me.

Dave smiled with his big white teeth, and I noticed how thick his chin stubble was compared to my own meagre growth. I could count on my hands the number of times I'd shaved, while he looked like he'd been shaving since grade four.

He clapped a hand on my shoulder, checked his watch and said: Let's do this.

The descent was easier today as we'd worked out a good way to combat the darkness. Dave led with his big torch in one hand and his Glock pistol in the other; I was just behind him with a torch in each hand, which I pointed over the balustrade to the right, so that their beams shone around the next bend and onto the stairs below. Anna and Mini each had a pair of solar-charged garden lanterns. We moved down the stairs as one giant mass of light, a lighthouse only confined by the concrete walls around us.

Within an hour we had reached street level and I'd said goodbye to the others, shut the door of the police car and backed up – a little too quickly; the accelerator was really responsive compared to Dad's old Ford. The dead body from yesterday had still been on the road when we'd come out of the lobby, covered in a fresh coat of snow. Dave and I had spotted it first and tried to block out the view from the girls, but they'd probably seen it anyway.

I put the car in drive and drove south down Sixth Avenue, watching my friends wave goodbye in the rearview mirror, before I turned left onto West 47th Street. The way ahead was clear enough to navigate. I drove slowly, no more than twenty kilometres per hour, and took the detours around other cars very carefully. A few times the tyres of the police car lost traction in the snow, and twice I had minor fender-benders despite slamming on the brakes as hard as I could. The cars were all pointed my way and I realised I was breaking yet another traffic law – but hey, I thought, I'm in a police car, whaddya gonna do? I played with the FM radio but just got that woodpecker noise.

I slammed on the brakes at the intersection of 47th and Park Avenue, but the car kept moving under its own inertia and bumped against the roof of an overturned white van. I winced, half expecting the airbags to go off but they didn't – maybe police cars didn't have airbags. In the snow-coated streets the white van had been well camouflaged. I looked around for a while, afraid the noise would have alerted Chasers to my position. There was nothing. I got out of the car, leaving it running and the driver's door wide open. Just metres beyond the van was Park Avenue. What I'd failed to see from inside the car was the unexpected; before me was a veritable mountain. A building that had once stood on the corner of 47th and Park was now a snow-covered mass of rubble that stretched across the street. For a moment I wondered if I should get the gun out of the car, then swore to myself I'd only be thirty seconds as I climbed on top of the van to look around.

The road to the north was in ruins – it looked like a bomb had struck the two high-rises between 47th, 49th and the Waldorf Astoria, which was still standing on Park Avenue, a stubborn symbol of better times. This intersection was impassable.

I got off the van and quickly walked back to the car, imagining the whole time there was something behind me, creeping silently in the snow, hunting me down. I locked the doors, put the car in reverse, did a seven-point turn to bring it around and headed back along East 47th Street. I drove more quickly this time, then turned left onto Madison Avenue and headed south. I slowed and checked the map on the passenger seat, sometimes driving over the kerb and along the footpath, south to East 41st. At one point I used the car to push a cab out of the way; I gritted my teeth as it scraped along the passenger side. Less than a hundred metres further on I knew I'd come the wrong way; there was no getting around the pile-ups in this neighbourhood. I'd have to get out and walk.

I kept the car idling and looked around for a while, checking my mirrors constantly. There was plenty of petrol in the tank and I wasn't afraid to wait it out, ready to reverse off at the sight of anyone who'd heard me scraping my way past that cab. But the coast seemed clear. I imagined that as soon as I shut off the engine, Chasers would come out of nowhere and charge at me and I'd have to back all the way up Madison until I could turn around. I wondered if I could put the car into a hand-brake turn like people did in the movies. I checked my map for the fourth or fifth time, folded it and tucked it into a thigh pocket of my trousers.

Snow began to fall, lowering visibility – that was a good thing. A few deep breaths later, I turned off the ignition and got out.

It was freezing. I'd become so used to being in the car with the heater on full blast that I'd forgotten how cold it was. I considered getting back in the car, reversing up Madison and trying to head west and then south and circle back, but quickly dismissed it.

Yeah, I thought, as I pulled the FDNY jacket out of my bag, I could drive around for hours looking for a route to my destination when it was now just a few blocks away. Before leaving I pocketed the keys and checked the boot. It contained some traffic cones, two big, heavy riot-type kevlar vests, a medical pack and a box of accident roadside flares, which I took. My hand rested on the open lid for a while as I looked up and down the street. There were man-sized lumps in the snow. They reminded me of a book I'd read as a child, in which the adults in the story insist a drawing of a boa constrictor that has swallowed an elephant is just a hat. The mind sees what it wants to.

I took one vest out, shut the boot and headed south. The vest was heavy over my shoulder so I decided to put it on over my coat and then the backpack over that.

I was moving around like the Michelin man, but I felt bigger – safer and taller.

I walked south and snow began to fall in thick, silent sheets. Without the heat of a busy city or the snow ploughs, it settled where it fell, quickly becoming firm and ankle-deep. I looked up; the sky was heavy and dark. I thought of Anna, Mini and Dave in 30 Rock. I thought of watching DVDs and listening to music and drinking hot chocolate. I walked faster.

I realised we'd need to plan for future trips. There were heaps of cars around with keys in the ignition. I tried a few and found that only one in every five or six still started – mostly the taxis and police cars, but also a couple of vans. I began lifting up their passenger-side windscreen wipers. I hoped I'd be able to come back and do this with my friends – check which cars still worked and mark them on a map, like I was doing now. Maybe we could even catalogue them in more detail – record how much petrol each one had, what kind of cars they were. Park a few good ones close to our building.

I came across a few courier motorbikes, but they either wouldn't start or were too heavy to push upright on my own. I also found a scooter with half a tank of petrol – you could probably run around the city all day on that. For a second I thought about taking it but then realised it would probably slow me down – there were too many places where the road was impassable, even for such a small vehicle. Plus, it was actually noisier than most of the cars I'd started. I'd hate to be on it and not hear a Chaser approaching me, or be surprised by another mountain of rubble and have to get off and walk anyway, having attracted every Chaser within earshot.

Still, it would have been a great thing to have in 30 Rock, for mucking around with on the roof, but there'd be no way I'd get it up all those stairs. Pity.

Thinking about our temporary home I checked my watch: almost three o'clock. I'd been moving far too slowly, spending time messing around with cars. I knew I should start heading back, do the rest of this trek tomorrow at first light. I'd never been afraid of the dark before, but since the subway . . . I didn't want to be trapped out here. Not in the dark. Not alone.

Despite the time, I decided to continue on for a bit longer. As I walked eastward along 40th its buildings seemed to bear down on me. I climbed over wrecks of cars, scrambled over rubble, around a crater. At the corner of 40th and Second Avenue I stopped and took off my pack and had a sip of water. As I put the bottle back I saw the Glock and pulled it out—

Scurrying behind me. Squirrels? No; rats, two of them, darting past me. Across the street I saw my reflection in a window but it didn't look like me. I saw a man in a big fire coat and a kevlar vest, and although I couldn't make out the gun in his hand I knew it was there. I practised bringing it up into a two-handed aim at my reflection. I did this three times—

More rats. At least eight or ten, a group of them running past me in almost the same direction as the last group. Those little critters were organised. I looked around to see where they were running from and saw another group of rodents. There must have been thirty or more, dark browns and black-greys against the brilliant white snow, and before they were past me I heard a new noise. A rumbling. It grew in volume to the point where it was as if I was in the middle of a thunderstorm.

I watched as a building came down on the other side of Second Avenue, the only major building on the block between 41st and 40th, falling as if in slow motion. Not that it was slow – in under five seconds it had fallen into itself like a house of cards coming down to a rapid drumbeat soundtrack. Before the dust started billowing out I was blown off my feet and flat on my back. I couldn't breathe. The noise of the final moment of the building's collapse was deafening and I shut my eyes and covered my face with my hands to protect it from the debris. I lay there for several minutes, trying to catch my breath.

At last I stood, bending over at first to cough up some grit, then I straightened up and started, swinging the pistol towards a figure in the shop window. It took me a few seconds to recognise myself – I looked like a ghost. I was covered in powdered concrete from head to toe; only my face was partially clear.

I trudged on in the snow, more slowly now, the gun heavy in my hand, snow on my shoulders, dust still clogging the air, and twenty minutes later I realised I'd walked without taking in my surroundings. I felt sick with fear of the unknown. All I wanted to do was to sit down and rest and maybe sleep until all this passed. Then maybe I'd wake up and things would be normal again. Better than normal. Mum wouldn't have left and Dad wouldn't have married anyone else; I'd sleep in on weekends and hear Mum and Dad laughing from the kitchen; I'd go fishing with Dad and it would be summer and we'd never leave each other or fight about anything.

Minutes later I reached the Queens Midtown Tunnel and was shocked back into reality. The tunnel was impassable and I saw things inside – horrific things – that

I hope I won't ever have to talk about. Thousands of people must have tried to escape Manhattan here, but fire had claimed them and it was a death worse than anything I could have imagined. There was still some heat coming off the smouldering plastic and rubber and fuel, and the smell sent me away faster than the sight.

I ran blindly south, the gun held high, wishing I could confront the people responsible for all this. I threw up two blocks later and there was some blood amongst the bile and I heaved until I was dry and my eyes watered. I washed my face and mouth with water from my bottle, then started moving again. My legs felt heavy, my pack too. I was exhausted. I walked in the snow and I was alone and I wanted nothing more than to shoot whoever had done this.

11

I walked slowly across Stuyvesant Oval, forgetting where I was or what I was doing, listening to my feet crunch in the snow. The sound reminded me of something from my childhood, but the memory was so faint it disappeared before I could grab hold of it. On the other side of the oval was a maze of brick apartment blocks that looked uniform, but not in a crappy, fake, *Truman Show* kind of way – these were big tall totems, built around the mid-twentieth century. Maybe earlier. The trees out front looked like they were upside down, their bare branches splayed out like roots reaching for life, each one separating into ever smaller offshoots. I knew there was a name for patterns that reproduced themselves like this, but after five minutes I still couldn't think of it and then I got fed up because I was spending too much time in my mind.

I sat on the edge of a small frozen fountain and opened my bag, and discovered a little book tucked in the side. I was surprised but in another way I'd almost been expecting it. *Siddhartha* by Hermann Hesse. I opened it and there was a note tucked inside the front cover, from Anna: *This is my dad's favourite book and he read it when he was your age. Good luck and come back soon. A.*

Her writing reminded me of my own but it was neater, as if she wrote slowly and deliberately. Her letter A was a simple, nice touch and I remembered how her lips had felt on mine. Straightaway I felt guilty for even thinking about it. Maybe it was a reaction to extreme stress – the desire to be close to someone after witnessing all that death. Thinking about my friends made me wish they were here, sitting by me in the cold, but I knew I had to do this alone.

As more snow fell I moved to the steps under an apartment block's awning and looked more closely at the book's cover. It had a picture of someone wearing a yellow headscarf, sitting in a little boat among some water lilies. The boat might have been in a river or the sea. No, it would have to have been still water with the lily pads sitting there like that, undisturbed but for the passage of the boat. I tucked the book into my jacket's side pocket, the gun hanging heavy in the other, and pulled the hood up over my head.

As I headed east between the vacant buildings I kept asking myself: Why? Why did this happen? With each footfall in the snow, I thought: Why, why, why? Then: Who? The Russians? North Koreans? Chinese? French? The CIA? I laughed. Musing in this way was a sign that perhaps I was becoming as crazy as the people who'd done this. Clearly what had happened here was the act of madmen. Smashing apart a city, blowing it up and infecting the survivors . . . Who would want to hurt so many ordinary people? There could be no reason for this kind of attack, no justification.

I exited Stuyvesant onto Avenue C and stopped to check my map. I was close to the East River. I considered entering one of the nearby apartment buildings and heading to the roof for a view of the river, but the thought of walking up a dark stairwell without my friends . . . Despite their warnings I decided to take a risk and go to the riverbank. It was really close and I'd come so far. I had to know for Dave – for all of us – if the bridges were still standing.

I tucked the map away and held the Glock in my hand as I walked east. The snow was still falling steadily and I reasoned that if there were any Chasers at the river they wouldn't be able to see any further than I could. The wind was stronger as I neared the water, and the powdery snow billowed and eddied around me, stinging my face. I wondered if I'd have Dave's courage if I was confronted by a Chaser. I wondered if even he would have the courage to do it again.

In less than five minutes I'd reached the spot where East 25th Street ended. I took a pedestrian passage under FDR Drive and came out to see a small, grassed strip that was fenced off from the East River. It was empty: not a Chaser, animal or person in sight. The water was misty and I waited there in the cold until the view cleared. From this position, according to the map, I'd have a good view to the south.

What I saw when the snowfall eased made my heart sink. I felt Dave's distress and disappointment as if he were right there with me. I was glad he wasn't – I didn't want him to see what I was seeing.

The Williamsburg Bridge was down. The big supports were still intact, but the middle span was a mess of twisted road that plunged into the water. A sailboat was on the river, moving aimlessly like it had broken its moorings. I watched as it drifted slowly, taken by the current—

A noise. I cocked my head to the side and listened harder, but I couldn't hear anything apart from the sound of the wind and the lapping water.

There it was again; a shuffling sound. Coming from the tunnel under FDR Drive.

I ran a few paces to get a look. Someone was coming. They were just a shape in the darkness, a silhouette against the light at the end of the tunnel, moving towards me at a fast, rhythmical pace. The gait of the damned; the stride of a Chaser.

I pulled the slide back on the Glock; a round was already chambered so a bullet fell to the ground. Part of me wondered why I didn't just throw the gun into the river behind me. Instead, my finger found the trigger guard. It felt familiar, dangerous.

The figure was nearing. Soon I'd see his face. I tried to keep my hands steady and thought about firing some shots as a warning over the head of the advancing—

Boy.

No more than my age. Same height and size, an average-looking teenager. His features were gaunt and pale, like he was malnourished and tired. A refugee from a war zone.

'Stop!' I shouted. I had a vision of the man Dave had shot and my finger tightened around the trigger. I could do this. If he came any closer I would shoot. 'Stop!'

He kept advancing towards me. My hands shook. His eyes moved, but he wasn't looking at me, he was looking at the East River behind me. It was as if he didn't even notice me. He passed me, not five paces away, scaled the fence, went to the water's edge and dipped his hands in. He scooped up the frigid water and brought it to his mouth. At the first taste he spat it out violently, a reaction to the salinated river. When he'd stopped gagging, he stood and gazed at the water as longingly as I imagined I would gaze at a rescue boat.

He turned back then and looked at me. His eyes bore no expression, absent like Mr Lawson's had been. He kept his gaze fixed on me as he crossed back over the fence and headed towards me. He looked so frail up close, like the wind would blow him over. His face was sunken, his cheekbones pronounced. Maybe he hadn't eaten since the attack.

'Stop there! Don't come any closer.'

I kept the gun pointed at him and took a couple of steps back, but his eyes stayed locked on mine. I wondered if he'd heard me, or if I'd even spoken out loud. I'd been on my own for a while; maybe I was forgetting how to talk?

He was one step away from me. When he reached out, I raised my arm to stop him and he fell backwards. He got up slowly and reached for me again; I pushed him harder this time and he stumbled over and lay still in the snow. He didn't seem to have the strength to get up. I felt a rush of pity for him.

I put the Glock in my pocket and pulled out the water bottle from my backpack, unscrewed the cap and bent down to the boy. I could almost imagine him as my brother. I held the bottle to his lips and he didn't resist or flinch; he let the water fill his mouth and held it there for a while, watching me as he swallowed. His eyes never left mine as I tipped more of the liquid into his mouth, then picked up his hands and held them to the bottle. With my action something seemed to register in him, something he'd forgotten how to do, and he propped himself up in the snow and drank just enough to wet his mouth. His eyes never left mine and they broke my heart as I wondered, *Who are you?*

I took out an apple and bit it and put the juicy flesh against his mouth. His eyes went wide and he sucked on the cut fruit but didn't seem to know to bite it. His hands were shaking and the tips of his fingers were black and it's not without shame and regret that I left him there, bare against the elements. His future and mine, I knew as I walked back through the tunnel under FDR Drive, were linked. He was what could have been and what might still become of me: a shell, a body that humanity had abandoned but for occasional rare encounters with others. *The kindness of strangers*, I heard Anna's voice say in my mind. She was starting to sound more and more like the books she read, while Mini sounded like the DVDs we watched and Dave just grew more silent, speaking only when he was angry and saying the things I wished I could say for myself. In a way we all spoke for one another, and as I walked fast towards where I'd left the police car I hoped there would be enough light left in the day to find my way back home to 30 Rock.

12

The darkness of a winter afternoon surrounded me as I sat in the police car. I took off my wet shoes and socks and sat there with the engine running and the heater on. The windows fogged up and I added the air con, pumping the heat to full. I kept the lights off and spent fifteen minutes flicking through the radio bands. For the first time I heard something being transmitted – one of the AM stations was playing faint, crackling music, the unmistakable voice of Billie Holiday. It took a few minutes before I realised it was pre-recorded; the song was on a continuous loop. I imagined some place in the mountains where an automated radio station was doing its thing.

I couldn't make up my mind whether to drive or not. The snow had picked up again, making it hard to see. If I put on the headlights and the beams started bouncing off the other cars all the way home, I'd be a magnet for bad guys. But if I stayed out here in the car all night, all alone . . . I decided to wait and see if the snow eased enough for me to navigate my way safely back to 30 Rock.

Someone had been through this area since I'd left it earlier – there was a big dumpster on its side in the middle of the road, not far from the police car. When it came time to leave I'd have to use the car to push it out of the way. It looked heavy – I'd have to accelerate and hit it really hard. I sized the dumpster up in the rear-view mirror and started to hate it for being in my way. I looked forward to smashing it.

I ate an apple and three packets of nuts – cashews, my favourite. I wondered which of my friends had packed them in there for me. I looked around the police car. I knew every inch of my surroundings despite it being almost totally dark.

By the time night fell, I might as well have been in a submarine stuck on the ocean floor for all I could see outside. I shone the wind-up torch at the fuel gauge and saw there was about two-thirds of a tank left. The heater had warmed me up and my clothes were now dry so I switched off the engine for a bit. I would stay put until the snow stopped falling. I nestled under the warmth of my dry clothes and tried to sleep. At home, before all of this, I used to think about the fact that I could never remember my dreams and wonder if life itself was just a dream. If that was true, why had it turned into a nightmare?

The car rocked and I woke.

I wiped saliva from the corner of my mouth and wondered for a moment where I was. For a second I thought I was a young kid again, asleep in the backseat of the car. I looked around, expecting to see my dad, but my eyes settled on the shiny Glock instead. I'd left it on the dashboard. The inside of the car had fogged up, but it seemed lighter outside than in. Moonlight, I supposed. I reached for the door handle—

At the last second I pulled back my hand. The car was still rocking a little on its shockers. Something had bumped into it. Or deliberately pushed it. My stomach clenched into knots as I remembered that was what had woken me.

My body wouldn't move. I closed my eyes, hoping that when I opened them again I'd be somewhere else, or maybe still asleep. But I couldn't fool myself.

I watched the water in the bottle on the passenger seat vibrate. Every muscle in me ached and I sat there watching my breath steam in the chill air until the water in the bottle was still. I used my sleeve to wipe away a small section of condensation on the window. Outside, the moon was bright against the white snow. I couldn't see anyone – couldn't see who or what had bumped into the car. I wondered if it could have been something else, the aftershock of a building falling down, perhaps. The thought gave me the briefest moment of relief until I heard crashing noises coming from the road behind me.

I tasted bile in the back of my throat, then bent over and threw up on the passenger seat floor. Cold sweat beaded my face and neck. I had to stay down. I wiped my mouth and quickly checked my watch; it was just after midnight. I could hear more noises outside; it sounded like a pack of people were trawling through the big overturned dumpster. Maybe they weren't Chasers? Maybe they were survivors, like me, looking for . . . But why would they go through the rubbish? There were literally thousands of shops that could be looted for untouched food. Only Chasers lacked the sense to walk into an abandoned convenience store and open up the fridge to a lifetime's supply of drinks.

I half pulled back the slide on the Glock and saw there was a round in the chamber, ready to fire. It was a confident move and it reminded me of something Dave might do. I looked out the window at the cars on Madison Avenue. I could see eight vehicles and none had their windows fogged up like mine, which meant that my car would stand out like a beacon to anyone looking for survivors. I gulped and made a small, strange sound in the back of my throat. I tasted blood.

There was an odd scraping noise, big and loud, as if the dumpster was being pushed along the road. I started to gently wind down my window—

There was a loud growling noise, and before I knew it the view in front of my eyes was obscured and the car began to rock again.

I started the ignition – the heater and air con blasted out on high – but before I could put on the headlights or move into gear, something registered. In that blink of an eye, through the narrow gap in the window, I had seen not a person but something much bigger. Something that didn't make sense in New York City.

I switched on the lights and the windscreen wipers. In front of me, past the stack of cars that were smashed together in a pile-up, was a massive white bear. It had its face turned towards the headlights so I dimmed them and wiped the inside of the windscreen for a better look. The animal watched me, then ambled over to forage in the dumpster.

I reached into my bag and pulled out the last few pieces of fruit. Without stopping to consider whether polar bears ate fruit or sixteen-year-old boys, I opened my door, walked out to where a car separated us and tossed an orange and banana towards it. They thumped to earth in the snow and the bear rose up on its hind legs but otherwise didn't move. It only sniffed the air, then stood there with steam snorting from its nose. I wondered what it made of all of this. Maybe the city was better for the bear this way: empty, so it could roam around as it pleased. Sniffing the air towards me again, the bear let out a deep growl, then turned and trudged down Madison on all fours, a massive presence on the white snow.

I'd felt strangely safe with the bear, but now it had gone I was gripped by panic again. I walked to the still-running car, got in and locked the driver's door.

The bear had cleared the way past the dumpster so I put the car in gear and drove north up Madison, turning left onto 42nd and passing the New York Public Library. I travelled back the way I'd come earlier, the route imprinted on my memory – all the way up Sixth and back around onto 49th and Rockefeller Plaza.

I parked the car as close to the entrance of 30 Rock as I could. When I switched off the headlights, it seemed darker than ever. Time was measured in heartbeats and it was ticking fast; I wondered if this fear inside me would ever leave. I told myself that what I imagined was out there in the cold dark night was worse than the reality. Chasers were human and they were probably weaker than I was; I could outrun them if I had to.

I pulled the key from the ignition. It took me another hundred heartbeats to drum up the courage to unlock the door and get out. Without looking left or right, I bolted into the foyer and up the stairs. It was only when I reached the fourth floor that I stopped to get my torch, my breath coming out in rasps and my heart feeling like it might explode.

Shining the light up the stairs, I continued to climb. At the 21st floor, I stopped again and rested, remembering the first time we'd stopped here.

I knew in volunteering to do this trip I had wanted to prove something to the others: that I could do it alone. But I was so tired. I was tired and my torch beam was nothing against the gnawing fear that made me afraid of shadows, and I wished that Dave was there with me.

I tried to imagine that he was. I saw his bright friendly eyes and big smile and pictured us laughing together as we climbed, and it was the only thing that got me up the remaining flights of stairs.

13

I couldn't get back to sleep again for a long time
that night. Thankfully the others couldn't either; the
three of them were awake when I got back, wanting to
know every detail of what I'd seen. I told them about the
Williamsburg Bridge first and surprisingly Dave didn't
seem too upset; it was almost as if he'd been expecting
it. I told them about the bear, about the cars I'd marked,
about the falling building and the tunnel and the wrecks
outside. I left out what I'd seen inside the tunnel, and I
didn't tell them about the boy. I didn't quite know why,
but I wasn't ready to talk about him yet.

What should we do now? Anna said.

Have you seen anything else? I asked.

No, nothing, Anna replied. Sorry.

I wondered what they'd got up to while I'd been gone. Part of me suspected they'd done nothing. It's not as if I'd been expecting much, but I hoped that maybe they'd have some news for me. A sighting. Something they'd found.

I saw a boat floating down the East River, I told them, remembering the sailboat bobbing along in the water.

Anyone on it? Dave asked.

Doubt it, I said. It was just drifting along with the current.

We could get a boat, Anna said. We'd be safer out on the water, at least from Chasers. We could sail to another city.

We'll check the maps tomorrow, Dave replied. There's a couple of spots where they have heaps of boats—

Like that Boat Basin, I cut in, remembering our first day in town when we'd had lunch on West 79th Street. I'd been sitting at a table with Anna and Mini and another guy, when Dave had come over to say hello and ended up joining us. He'd been funny that day, and the four of us had been so involved in our conversation that we hadn't noticed the rest of the group had moved on to do the tour of Midtown.

It sounds like a good idea, Dave said slowly. But can any of us handle a boat? I mean, maybe we should stick to dry land. We could find an SUV and stock it up, head north out of Manhattan.

I'd prefer to be on the water than the road, I said. Especially at night. It's not secure sleeping in a car – not with Chasers out there. A boat would be better, but yeah, we'd need to figure out how to work it.

Where would we go? Anna asked. I mean, what direction? Upriver?

Maybe, Dave replied. Or maybe along the coast; head north towards Boston, look for refugees out of town.

That's the direction those jets were flying on that first day, I said.

Memories of the first moments after emerging from the subway started to flood back, so I said quickly: In the morning we should make a list.

A list?

Yeah, places that we could go, how we might get there. Help us make a choice – we can't stay here like this forever.

We can take our time making a decision though, right? Mini said. We don't want to get this wrong. We have a good set-up here.

We can't wait for someone to fix this, Dave said. If we want out, we gotta do it ourselves.

Yeah, but there's no rush, is there? Mini said. We have almost everything we need here, it's comfortable. Right?

That's true, Min, I said gently. But it would be good to make some plans, just in case.

I guess, Mini said. I do like having choices.

My dad used to say that no matter what happens, it's the one thing you're always left with, I said.

You sound like you think this is it, Dave said. Like you think we're the only survivors who aren't infected and it's up to us to start things over again.

Like a new earth, Anna said.

I looked at her. A new earth?

It's like the planet has reset, she explained, to create a new earth full of hope. Those of us who are left will become the adults of a world that's changed, a world where things like wars and greed are just a memory . . . It's like the torch has been passed to a new generation.

Maybe this is what happens to cultures every now and then, I said. It's like starting afresh—

What, you think there's been some massive attack like this before? Dave said. I mean, the world wars were big but in reality only a small portion of the world's population was killed. This . . . this could be billions of people. This could be everyone but us. We have no idea.

I didn't mean that, Anna said. What I meant was there have been places where the whole population has seemed to vanish. Like Easter Island. It happens. For whatever reason, this kind of stuff happens.

And the Mayans, I added. They had whole cities that were abandoned and forgotten for centuries.

We lay there in silence and I looked out at the skyline of a city that just days ago was one of the busiest places on earth. The city that never sleeps was now a cold bed.

Maybe this new earth is hell, Dave said. Maybe we're in hell. Those people out there, the Chasers, they're in purgatory. And for us . . . for us, it's inevitable: we'll end up there too.

I doubt it, I replied and it came out louder than I'd intended.

What, you been an angel all your life? Dave said.

Me? No, but I don't think I've done anything to go to hell over. And I know you guys wouldn't be in hell. The people who did this? They're the ones who'll wind up there, in hell or whatever you want to call it.

There was silence for a long time and I heard Mini's breathing grow deep and even.

Tomorrow, I'm going to beef up security, Dave said in a low voice. We need better fallback plans, especially once we leave here; more weapons, just in case.

How do you know all this stuff? Anna asked.

Play Station, Dave said. XBox.

Anna snorted.

Good idea, Dave, I said.

Way I see it, we gotta keep this building secure until we leave, Dave said.

When will that be? Mini asked, and her quiet voice made me jump. I thought she'd fallen asleep.

Soon enough, Min, I said, not sure if she'd heard what we'd just been talking about.

Okay, she said sleepily. But don't leave without me. Don't forget me.

Within minutes she was breathing deeply again.

A storm rolled in just before dawn and the sound of the wind and rain, even through the thick glass of the skyscraper, was calming. As I fell asleep, I wondered why Min would have said what she did; I hoped I'd never forget any of them.

14

I found my Spiderman suit hanging over the back of a restaurant chair when I woke up. It had been cleaned and I couldn't remember if I'd washed it before I left the previous day or if one of my friends had done it. I put on the suit, then pulled on a T-shit and jeans for extra warmth.

Mini was still asleep but Dave and Anna were nowhere to be seen. I hoped they were on the observation deck, checking out the city for activity. I went to the storeroom behind the bar, took a can of Coke from a massive wall of soft drinks and went upstairs.

Dave was on the outside deck of the 67th floor, rugged up against the cold and using the binoculars to scan the south. I called out to him that I was going to clear some more rooms and he gave me a wave and a thumbs-up.

I headed downstairs again, stopping in the Rainbow Room to get my room-clearing kit: Dave's fire axe, my Glock, a powerful torch and a tool-belt. I tucked the gun and torch in the tool-belt and continued down to the 59th floor. This level was fairly boring to clear – mainly a couple of big offices with nothing much of use, unless I wanted to start up my own insurance agency one day or a terrible-looking publishing venture of brochures and catalogues. I caught my reflection in a foyer mirror and saw I was quite a sight: a superhero-turned-handyman, packin' a pistol. I did a couple of quick-draws and then put it away, remembering there was a round in the chamber. I wondered if Anna was somewhere on this floor and what she'd think of my get-up.

There were four apartments on the western side of this level and I used our 'master key' – Dave's fire axe – to gain entry to apartment 59C. The wood around the handle of the door splintered and gave way on the fifth swing so I leaned the axe against the wall and went inside. I was used to breaking and entering now; used to eating other people's food and wearing their clothes. It wasn't something I would have done a week ago, but I figured there was now a different set of rules.

The apartment was dark throughout so I opened the timber blinds. Beyond the entry was the lounge room. There were piles of books everywhere and a few stuffed animals mounted on the walls – even the head of a brown bear. I remembered the bear from last night and hoped it would never end up like this. Maybe killing animals for fun would never happen again. Maybe Anna was right and this was a new earth.

In one corner of the lounge was a display case that housed a few ornaments and a medal, which turned out to be a Nobel Prize for literature.

The first room off the hallway was a study, a big oak-panelled room with books stacked neatly on floor-to-ceiling bookshelves. I ran my fingers along the spines, thinking that later in the day I'd carry a stack of old novels up to the Rainbow Room to add to Anna's collection. She was spending more and more time reading and writing in her journal, which I guess was a good thing because it seemed to make her happy, but it also meant that she was quiet and I was beginning to miss the sound of her voice.

On the desk was an old-fashioned typewriter, the kind I'd only ever seen in movies. The desk itself looked antique too – it was old and wooden with a well-worn green leather top. I sat on a swivel chair that squeaked and creaked as I spun around, then tried punching out a few lines on the typewriter. The keys were stiff and hard to use – nothing like my laptop back home.

I left the study and checked out the fridge in the kitchen. There was no off smell when I opened the door, as there had been in some of the other apartments. I shone the torch inside and discovered this was because there was no perishable food of any kind, no fruit or vegies or meat. There were a few jars of condiments, but aside from that there was just a whole range of drinks – bottled water, juices, mixers, soft drinks, beer, white wine. I found another low, two-door fridge under the kitchen bench, full of more booze and mixer drinks. The walk-in pantry was stocked with enough canned food and packets of flour, rice and pasta to last someone a couple of years, maybe more. I wondered about the kind of person who would stockpile so much food.

I helped myself to a packet of chocolate biscuits and ate them as I wandered through the rest of the apartment. There was one bedroom, which was big and opulent and full of antique furniture. It had a great view to the west; the buildings of Manhattan looked like a vast man-made Lego village. In the wardrobe I found racks and racks of clothes that looked like they belonged to an old guy. Funny, I thought, there are no photos in this apartment, not one.

There was another room that could have been used as a bedroom but there was no bed, just a messy stack of boxes. I had a quick look through them and found women's clothes and a box of wigs. In one of the last boxes I opened there were some photos, most of them black-and-white. They showed a couple on their wedding day and then on holidays and at parties. I wondered if she'd left him and that was why all her clothes were boxed up, but quickly realised that her things wouldn't still be here if she had. It made me sad to think what had become of her, so I put the photos away and left the room.

Beyond the two bedrooms was a linen closet that was stocked with half-a-dozen giant water bottles, the kind you put in water coolers. They were all full and I made a mental note to tell the others – they might come in handy one day.

The last door in the hallway wouldn't open. It seemed weird to have a locked door inside an apartment, and weirder still when I realised there was no visible lock. I tried again; the handle turned but the door wouldn't budge. It must be locked from the inside, I thought. Must have a slide-across bolt or something . . . It took a few seconds for the gravity of this to hit me: *the door was locked from the inside.*

My hand moved to the Glock in my tool-belt and I drew it slowly, careful not to make a sound. I stood with my ear pressed against the door, trying to decide whether to shoot it open or go back and get the axe. I felt sick with fear. I didn't want to turn my attention away from the door and whoever might be behind it, so finally I slid my finger in the trigger and pointed the gun at the door handle.

15

A loud bang like a gunshot woke me and I sat up, breathless.

It was light, the dull morning light of another overcast day. My sheets and T-shirt were soaked with sweat and I sat on the edge of my bed, my forehead resting on my hands. I had a splitting headache and my mouth was dry. I looked around and saw my Spiderman suit hanging over the back of a restaurant chair. The sight of it confused me, but then I smiled as I realised that finding apartment 59C, the photos, the locked door – everything – must have been a dream.

I heard someone stirring and saw Mini in her makeshift bed. It surprised me; I'd thought her bed was empty. Then I noticed Anna and Dave sitting at the table. Dave was reading an old newspaper and drinking coffee, and Anna was having tea and reading Jane Austen. I laughed with relief.

I took a change of clothes to the men's room and washed with yesterday's cold washcloth. I soaped up and rinsed my hair in a bucket of water, and returned to the others feeling more alive and hopeful than I'd felt in days.

Mini was sitting up in bed and rubbing sleep from her eyes. She pretended not to notice me as I went over and sat at the table with Anna and Dave. I helped myself to a bowl of cereal, pouring out a small carton of long-life milk. I sat crunching my cornflakes and looking outside at the clouds as they swirled and thinned.

I was about to ask Anna to pass me the juice when I stopped cold. The sweat was back. There, by Dave's plate, was the Nobel medal.

Where did you get that? I said.

Dave saw me staring at the medal and shrugged. I found it in some apartment yesterday, he said and went back to reading his paper.

Which one? I asked.

No answer.

Dave, which one?

Which one, *what*?

He didn't bother looking at me as he read, the paper a wall between us.

Which apartment did you find it in?

Some apartment on level 59 – I don't know which one, it was full of weird crap.

Like what?

Just like old-school crap.

Stuffed animals?

No doubt, he said. He looked over his paper and eyed me like I was annoying him.

Yeah, there were stuffed animals, he went on. It was kinda like an old-school hunting lodge; old rifles on the wall, plenty of old books and stuff. Like from another time.

Anna glanced up from her book to listen in.

But the medal, I said. Where'd you find the medal?

What's with you?

I just want to know – was it in a case?

You all right?

I just looked at him.

Yeah, he said. It was in a glass case, some kind of display thing in the lounge room. What's with you this morning – you not sleep well?

Did this apartment have an office – a study?

Yeah, he said. It had a study.

He gave Anna a look like I'd gone nuts, and she just shrugged and went back to reading her book. I wanted to shake the information out of Dave to prove to Anna that I wasn't crazy.

This study have a desk?

Don't most studies? Dave said.

An antique desk with a green leather top and an old black typewriter with stiff keys and a chair that—

And a chair that squeaked, yeah, Dave said.

And there was a bedroom with a good view to the west and another room full of boxes and a linen closet and—

And a door at the end of the hallway that was locked, Dave said.

He leaned back, finally looking interested. The girls were now also listening closely to our conversation.

What is it? Mini asked as she sat down at the table.

The front door to that apartment was deadlocked, Dave said. I cut around the lock with the fire axe. You must have gone in there afterwards, Jesse.

Or maybe there's another apartment just like it? Anna suggested.

No, I said. It was that apartment. I dreamed I was in there, yesterday, then woke up just as I smashed through the door at the end of the hallway and . . .

And? Mini asked. Her eyes were locked on mine and they were as wide as saucers.

What did *you* do, Dave? I said.

Sorry?

What did you find in there? I asked. What did you see in that room?

He stared at me, his expression puzzled and then annoyed as he realised he'd have to explain himself. He folded his paper and leaned forward. When he spoke it was in the tone my uncle always used when he told off my cousin and me.

I told you about all this yesterday afternoon, he said. Don't you remember? I told you about it, gave Anna a stack of books, and brought up a few bottles of juice. You wore this stupid medal all through dinner, which was the chicken Mini got from the roof, but it made you sick and you went to bed early.

I looked at the others. Anna gave a little nod over the top of *Pride and Prejudice* and went back to reading. Mini looked worried for me and Dave had a big stupid grin on his face like he was glad I was losing my marbles.

Sorry . . . I must be going nuts, I said. I looked out the window and strained to replay my dream, but I could only remember up to the locked door. I could picture every detail of that door. Am I such a coward that I've started living my life through Dave's adventures?

Dave checked his watch; it looked like one I'd taken out of someone's apartment for myself, but then everything was starting to blend together.

Anyway, he said, I'm gonna head out. Do a little scouting.

Anna looked worried and shot me a glance.

Where are you going to go? she asked.

Gonna scout around for good vehicles, he replied. Might see if there's a way clear to the Boat Basin on West 79th. It'll give us options. And don't worry about me – if he can go out there and come back, so can I.

Fine, I said.

Fine? Anna sounded upset. How can you say that? She got up and stalked into the kitchen.

Dave gave me a smile that could have meant anything, so I said: Just try and be back before dark.

Yeah, he said, as if it was obvious. Look, I want to find out some stuff, like if we had to, could we drive outta here? Drive until we find help?

Drive until the roads are too clogged to go any further – then what, sleep in the car? Mini asked. We'll be dinner for them!

Meals on wheels, I joked.

Mini looked shocked and I shrugged in apology. Dave seemed annoyed that I wasn't taking his idea seriously.

We could get an SUV, he explained. A diesel four-wheel drive that can handle going off-road or nudging stuff out of the way. We can get heaps of spare gas, supplies, strap a few spare wheels to the roof.

Spare wheels from where?

Take them off cars of the same type, he said. We could drive inland, upstate, head for some towns up north, maybe towards Boston.

Anna heard the last of his plan as she returned to the table.

I'm not sleeping in a car with them out there! she said. What if we get stuck? No way am I going to be trapped in a car at night.

I remembered the polar bear. I thought we'd be safer with it around – safer from Chasers, anyway. It would sniff them out and warn us, maybe scare them off.

We can sleep in shifts, drive twenty-four seven, Dave reasoned aloud. Or we could park and hole up each night in a different place, a different house or apartment.

And what if all we find is more of *them*? Then what? Anna said. If we drive and drive we'll only be stuck in some hick town with whatever food we could fit in the car.

Boston's not exactly—

Shut up, Jesse, Anna said.

Mini shot me a sympathetic look. Dave seemed to be losing whatever spark he had for his idea.

Think of all the scary movies you've ever seen, Anna said. Those people would have been fine if they'd stayed together and stayed put. If this place isn't too bad, why move? Why tempt the hand of fate when you don't have to? And what if we move and then help shows up back here? You know, Murphy's Law.

It was just an idea, Dave said. It's just . . . I'd like to see what's out there, beyond our horizon. Find someone else – there must be others out there, hiding, like us.

Then I said what no one else wanted to say: What if we find nothing?

There was silence. It seemed to stretch on for so long that I was afraid if I didn't hear my friends' voices soon they might never speak again.

Dave should go out, I said. It's the smart thing to do.

What's the point? Anna said, looking straight at me.

To figure out possible escape routes, whether by car or boat—

All the bridges and tunnels are probably impassable, Anna said, cutting me off. We've got all we need right here.

That might be true, Dave said, but I gotta know. I gotta see it with my own eyes.

I started to get the feeling Dave was envious of the day I'd spent out there alone in his city.

We made a pact to stick together, Anna said. Everything always starts to go wrong when the group breaks up.

But what if we *have* to break up one day? I asked. What if we're separated and we can't do anything about it? What if one or more of us can't stand it here anymore?

What if? Anna asked, and her voice sounded different from what I was used to, more mature. What if an airlift comes and sees our sign on the roof and picks up those who are here, but you're not here and then you come back and it's too late. What then, huh?

Look, I said, maybe that will happen. But that day is not here yet. It may never come. So we should check out some other places, explore more . . . But we'll do it together, we'll be careful. And right now, if Dave has to go and see some things for himself, I think he should. I think if it's something that he needs to do, then who are we to stop him?

Dave didn't look convinced by my speech but he seemed grateful anyway.

You went out alone, he said.

Look, mate, I'm with you on this, I said. I went out alone because I thought you should stay here with them, to protect them—

Since when have we been 'them'? Anna asked.

You know what I mean, I said. Dave's . . . Dave's a big guy who can handle himself and I'm not so sure I could protect you like he can. That's all I meant.

You did okay out there on your own, Mini said. And we were fine here. I agree with you, Jesse. Dave can go if he wants. We'll be fine.

Anna left the table again. Dave stood, picked up his bag and disappeared from the room, not bothering with a goodbye.

In some ways it was a relief to know that Dave was out there exploring the city, although I'm not sure the girls would have admitted that. I hoped he'd come back with routes and paths and ideas we'd not thought about before. Or with stories about massive groups of survivors in shelters, protected by authorities who knew what had happened. When he wasn't back by lunchtime I started to fear the worst and wonder if we'd be all right without him. I didn't want to even consider if I could survive without all of them.

We kept busy until sunset, creating our sign up on the roof. It was a good day for it; the sky was overcast but for once it didn't feel like it was about to drop down on us. By the time daylight faded, we were covered in yellow paint and stank of petrol from our handiwork. If someone flew overhead they would see a yellow 'HELP' sign, and if we heard them coming we'd be able to toss a flare into one of the tubs of rags we'd soaked in kerosene and butane. Sure, Dave was out there scouting for us, but I was up here getting organised, and by the time we'd cleaned up and gone into the kitchen to make dinner I knew we had options. I could taste it.

I felt surer about the outside world too. I'd faced one of them; I'd faced that boy. Maybe not all of the Chasers were bad. Maybe they weren't all killers. That boy wasn't.

I reckon a Chaser would still kill you if they needed a drink badly enough, Anna said, as if she was reading my mind.

We were back in the Rainbow Room, sitting at our usual table eating spaghetti with tomato sauce. It reminded me of the pasta sauce I cooked with my dad sometimes. I noticed Mini had hardly touched hers.

If they were desperate, Anna went on, if they really needed what you have inside you, then they'd kill.

I nodded in agreement and she gave me a brief smile over the table.

But no matter what they're like, we've still got choices, I said. We could stay here until help comes, or we could go. We *could* separate – what Dave's doing now proves that . . .

I frowned and checked my watch. Anna pretended not to notice.

The one thing we have left is choice, I said. And each other.

Anna tried to smile again but almost cracked. She stood up suddenly, went over to her bed and started reading by torchlight. Mini left the table too, and started scrolling through an iPod. I blew out all the candles except for one and took it with me to bed. I tried to read by the flickering light but my mind wandered to the others who'd been with us on the UN camp. If I'd had to choose people to stay with me after the subway it would have been these three.

Anna's light went out and my candle flickered alone in the dark.

He'll be back soon, Anna said.

Yeah, I replied.

I want to do something fun tomorrow, Mini said. All four of us. We could play drinking games – Dave would like that.

I'm sure he would, Min, I said and then started to laugh. The others joined in and we laughed so hard that when we finally stopped I couldn't remember why we'd started laughing in the first place.

I think Dave'll come back, I said to the others. Actually, I know he will. Sometime tomorrow.

16

We ate well the next morning. Anna cut up fresh fruit into a salad. I got some yoghurt and eggs from the snow-covered stash on the roof. The eggs were just on their use-by date so we scrambled up a whole dozen. I felt sorry that Dave had to miss out. We even had fresh bread, baked in a breadmaker we'd found at the back of someone's kitchen cupboard. It was a little doughy inside but no one complained. I think even Mini had seconds that morning.

We played Monopoly for a few hours, trying to take our mind off things. We used real cash. I'd never bothered to count it, but there was a duffle-bag full of notes from all the apartments we'd ransacked. There must have been a hundred grand or more. It made the game fun, although Mini was a shark; she went all out at every turn, buying every property she could and never bothering to save anything. Anna only seemed interested in saving up to buy the premium sites, and I kept landing on the Chance and Community Chest cards, which never turned out in my favour. When Anna bought Broadway I tried to land on it – I looked forward to pretending to be in pain when I had to pay her rent – but then I hit one of Mini's mid-range hotel properties and it cleaned me out of the game.

I spent a few hours going through apartments on the 57th and 58th floors. Part of me realised I was avoiding 59C, the apartment I dreamed about so vividly, but I wasn't ready to confront it yet.

Under someone's king-size bed, I found a plastic suitcase full of drugs. White, powdery stuff, as well as some bags of what looked like rock salt and some small blue pills. Dave might know what it all was.

When I showed it to Anna and Mini back in the Rainbow Room they reacted with a mixture of interest and shock. I left the suitcase on the bar.

You should throw that off the roof, Anna said.

Why?

Because what do we need it for? she said. You want to take drugs?

No, of course not, I said. I didn't add, *Not now. Maybe in, like, ten years, if this is all there is.* But I didn't want to think that way. These guys were all I needed.

Just get rid of it. We don't need drugs.

What about for medicinal purposes? I said. What if one of us is in serious pain, like we have to set a leg or something?

You know how to do that? Mini asked.

No, he doesn't, Anna said. And even if he did, how would you know what kind of drugs to use and how much, Jesse? Throw them out.

I looked at the case and thought through every reason for keeping a big stash of drugs like that. Finally I shook my head.

We might need them to trade with, I said. Maybe someone will want them and we might need what they have.

What?

I don't know . . . Who knows what's going to be valuable out there? I picked up a big stack of cash. This might be worthless for all we know.

Everyone was silent and Anna disappeared, probably to go bury her head in a book.

Keep that case, I told myself, just in case there's a final day. A day when we have to escape, a day we know we won't be coming back. It might help, one day a long time from now, if the others leave me or don't make it and I'm alone in the world. If I'm truly alone, I want choices.

I spent the afternoon upstairs on the observation decks looking out at the city. I watched a big explosion in Brooklyn somewhere, which vanished as quickly as it had appeared. I saw a small group of people – Chasers? Refugees? – running in the street. I imagined Dave down there, trying to talk to some of them.

I bounced a tennis ball against the wall, thinking about home. I wondered what Dad was doing right at that moment. It would have been the early hours of the morning in Australia, but maybe he was lying awake, as worried about me as I was about him. I'd never really considered a life without him in it until now.

When I went downstairs, Anna and Mini were laughing about something. The sight of them acting so normal was exactly what I needed.

I was just saying to Anna that it would be cool to get some amazing art for this place, Mini said as I sat down at the table. Anna smiled. She was back to her old self and I was glad the conversation about the drugs seemed to have been forgotten.

We could go to MoMA, I suggested.

No way, Anna said. All that risk for some Warhols or Van Goghs?

What risk? I joked as I started building a house of cards on the table. You think the curator will have turned into a Chaser?

I just don't want to take those kinds of risks over something aesthetic like art, she said. Food, petrol, shelter, yeah, but not art.

How about celebrity houses?

Sorry, Min?

We could check out celebrities' houses, she said. You know – actors, singers, sports stars . . .

That would be cool, Anna said. But how would we find out where they lived?

Good point, I replied, and turned to Anna: So you think it's worth taking risks for that but not art?

She shook her head.

I wouldn't take risks for art or celebs' houses or anything like that. It's just that we were talking about things we could do and places we could go in Manhattan since this city is basically ours now. Well, when the Chasers are gone. Can you imagine checking out all the penthouses in this city?

That would take a lifetime, Mini said. And it would start to get really boring.

Maybe one day though, I thought, adding a second level to my house of cards.

Okay, said Anna. New topic. What's the greatest band ever?

Mayday, Mini said.

What? Are they some crazy Taiwanese boy band or something? I said.

They're not crazy, Mini replied and I remembered she'd talked about them once before.

Radiohead, I said. Greatest band ever.

What about the Beatles? Anna said. They don't rate?

Okay, then, I said, Radiohead are the greatest band with all their members still . . . you know. How about you?

I don't know . . .

You started this, I said. Come on. Aside from your crappy pop stuff, what band ranks?

Muse.

Serious? I asked. I heard they'd turned into some kind of Mormon tribute band.

Aren't Mormons allowed to have heaps of wives? Mini asked. I'd like to marry a rich Mormon.

What?

Well, I wouldn't have to do much work if there were other wives.

Anna turned to Mini: You want to be one of multiple wives? Where's the respect in that?

I think they can only have one wife anyway, I said. The multiple wife thing is pretty old-school. But hey, Anna's got two mums, remember?

What's that like? Mini asked. I mean, is one of them, like, your dad?

Does it matter anymore?

Yeah, it matters, I said. I went to touch Anna's hand but she pulled it away.

Why wouldn't it matter? Mini asked.

She thinks maybe she won't see them again, I said.

We were silent. I tried to think of something to say, but I didn't know how I could convince Anna she'd get to see her family again when half of me didn't believe it myself.

Maybe Dave's a Mormon.

What, you want to marry Dave now, Min?

No . . . I just thought maybe he is.

How would you know just by looking at him? I said. Besides, I think he's Catholic.

What, you can spot that?

No, I can't.

No more than I can see much of anything, I thought. I pushed the deck of cards to the side and looked at the big tourist map we were using as a tablecloth.

We've got so many options right here, I said, scanning the notes in the legend. Come on, we've ruled out celebs' houses, what else?

Why don't we go to the Natural History Museum? Anna said.

Huh?

If we're going to hide out somewhere, that would be a cool place. Think about it, she said and there was a glint in her eyes that I hadn't seen for a while.

What about City Hall? I added, reading off the map. Or Gracie Mansion? Or the Police Plaza?

Or Liberty Island? Anna added.

Or Grand Cen— Mini stopped herself as she remembered. Oops, sorry.

That place was too open anyway, I explained. We need to be somewhere without too many openings, otherwise it won't be secure enough.

Wonder what Dave would think? Anna asked, and then came a voice—

Federal Reserve Bank or New York Stock Exchange,

Dave said. Those places are like fortresses, designed to be terror-proof.

He was smiling from ear to ear and Anna and Mini jumped up and gave him a hug. As he passed me he held out his fist homie-style for me to punch, but then pulled it away at the last second.

What's in the Federal Reserve?

Gold, he said as he took off his coat and sat down at the table. Biggest storage in the world.

Cool, I said, thinking that Dave looked bigger than ever, pumped up after his adventure in the outside world.

But what would we do with gold? I asked.

What do you mean?

Jesse thinks that maybe drugs will be more valuable to trade with, Anna said, rolling her eyes. I don't think he sees value in gold now, or cash for that matter.

No, it's—

I stopped and decided not to have that discussion with them again. Instead, I turned to Dave and said: Did you see anyone out there?

No.

You didn't see *anyone*? I asked.

No one, he said, taking off his shoes.

What did you see?

Cars. Bodies. A building come down.

As he spoke I could see my own memories play in my mind like a movie. A movie of destruction and death and not a lot else.

There wasn't much snow out, but there's heaps of rubbish and dark slushy ash.

Ash? Mini asked.

Yeah, from all the burnt stuff, Dave said. Remember the footage of nine-eleven? All that dust and crap that covered people?

Not really, Min said, but Anna and I knew exactly what he meant. There was a photo of it in one of the apartments below us. My thoughts turned to apartment 59C. I could picture myself crashing through that locked door. The image was like a knife in my skull – in and out, hot and sharp, there and then gone again just as quickly.

So what's the plan? Anna asked.

We need to talk about it, I said. We need to make the decision together.

But we'll be leaving here, yeah?

Anna looked at Dave, but for once I felt like I had the answers.

Yeah, we're leaving here, I said. Dave nodded.

Will we go tomorrow?

I shook my head. The day after. First, we pack, we get prepared, we rest.

I looked at each of my friends in turn.

The day after tomorrow, we go, I said.

17

That night Dave told us stories about his day and a half outside. They were mostly boring and tended to go nowhere, so after a while I left him to it and went up to the roof to get some air. Part of me suspected he'd just been hiding in the stairwell for all that time. His bag looked exactly the same, as if he hadn't eaten any food or used anything. Where was the proof of what he'd seen? If he *had* lied about going out, could I really trust him? Would he be there for me when I needed him?

As I looked out at the dark city, questions kept flooding my brain. If I doubted Dave, how much did the others trust me? How far would they be prepared to follow me? Dave had been the unofficial leader of our group, but after he shot the Chaser down on the street that seemed to change. I was starting to feel more and more responsible for my friends. For the first time I could understand why Mum left my dad and me if this was how she felt – overwhelmed by a sense of duty and constantly doubting herself. I didn't want a lifetime of uncertainty. Decisions had to be made.

It felt surreal being on the roof in the dark. It had been a few days since I'd done the rubbish run, and I felt like I was throwing my friends off that roof when I launched the heavy bags into the blackness that yawned below. The ruins of the ice-rink would swallow them up like a mouth in the earth that ate what I didn't want, and maybe the rotten food in there would one day grow into some kind of garden and the polar bear would walk through it, and it would be king again and maybe even have a family. I longed to see new life in this place, this new earth.

I threw the final bag with everything I had, but at the last moment I stumbled and almost swung myself off the edge with it. Feeling sick, I sat down, my feet hanging over the edge of the building and my hands firmly grasped on a cold rail, wondering what it would be like to fall. What was the worst that could happen? I wasn't afraid of the height because I couldn't see much further than my legs that dangled into the darkness. I leaned forwards a little and the wind pushed upwards against my face and hair. Would I float like a kite? Was this wind strong enough to carry me away? What would happen if I just let go? What if I gave myself a little push, an accidental launch into the abyss . . . ?

I tried to laugh but a strange sound came out, like a sob. Would I do it? When? When my friends were gone? When we ran out of water? If something happened, something I couldn't live with? I remembered the Chaser Dave had shot and the teenage boy down by the river and that locked door in apartment 59C . . . I had to leave this place. With or without them, I had to leave more than just this building.

I wiped tears from my eyes and heard a voice inside me say, *Suck it up*, and I stood and yelled at the world and all who had made it this way. I screamed and yelled and felt alive and—

I stopped.

A light.

A flash caught my eye from the window of a neighbouring building. I was seventy storeys up; it couldn't have been natural. I strained my eyes but could no longer see it. I told myself it was so small and insignificant and passing that it was probably nothing. One fleeting shaft of light on a dark, moonless night. I stood up and turned to leave—

It was back. I'd seen it in my peripheral vision: a wavering beam like a torch. There, but gone just as quickly. Still, I was sure it was a sign of life; no light inside a building at night in this time and place could mean anything else. I glanced behind me, almost expecting to see Dave there playing a trick, but the roof was empty; I was alone.

I raced down to the observation deck on the 67th floor and ran along the windows until I reached the spot where I thought I'd seen the light. I looked through the binoculars and waited. I felt sick and sad, expectant and anxious. If there was someone else out there, someone like me . . .

I stood searching every possible window, wondering if I should run down and tell the others. But what if I left and the light flashed again? I remembered a scene in a Hitchcock movie where a guy in a wheelchair thinks he's seen a murder in one of the neighbouring apartments. He watches the window night after night, only to realise that the murderer is sitting in the dark – watching *him*. For a moment I wondered if the light could have been a Chaser trying to trick us; trying to lure us out . . . No, it had to be another survivor.

I sat there, staring through the binoculars for hours, waiting for another sign of life. Eventually I must have fallen asleep because I woke with a start, cold and uncomfortable.

Anna was sitting next to me, and I wondered if that's what had woken me. I checked my watch; it was just after midnight. Anna's face was a blurry reflection in the window before me, a ghost in natural colours. There was no light across the way, only darkness. Anna didn't ask about my subdued state or what I'd been doing, and I didn't volunteer anything. We sat there in silence for a while, but it was as if I could read her thoughts.

Do we have to leave? she asked finally.

I couldn't answer her. It was a question I kept asking myself and I would never be comfortable with the answer.

Nothing will be the same if we leave.

I know.

We might not be together anymore.

I know.

We might separate.

I know.

End up in different places.

I know.

Forever this time.

A tear rolled down my cheek; I knew what she meant. She deserved to go and be free to have her life and be with her own Mr Darcy or whoever was right for her. Maybe she and Dave would end up together; maybe she had more in common with him anyway. I knew they shared something special that I'd missed out on, and for the second time that night I thought about taking the ultimate 'out'.

I know we might split up if we leave, I said, but I'm afraid that if we stay too long, we'll end up going our own paths anyway; that I might wake up one morning and you'll be gone.

Would you blame me? she asked softly.

I was silent. I gazed at the reflection of her pretty face; she held my heart in a look.

Come on, I said finally, getting up and holding out my hand. If it's going be our last day here tomorrow, let's make it a good one. Right now, we need our sleep.

18

There were things I needed to sort out before leaving 30 Rock. I wanted to say goodbye to some of the places that held memories, and despite my fears I knew I needed to see what was in apartment 59C. I'd miss this building but not all of it. I wanted to leave but part of me also just wanted to lie in bed and not get up again until help arrived and the city went back to normal.

We fixed breakfast and I woke Mini by sitting on the edge of her mattress and calling her name. We ate and drank in silence. Afterwards I packed a big hiking pack that I'd found in someone's apartment with a change of clothes and enough food to last about a week. I slipped a couple of torches in the massive side pockets – our original wind-up one and a powerful

Maglite – as well as rechargeable batteries, two iPods, a toothbrush, toothpaste and soap, a small medical kit, about a dozen gas lighters and matches, and a plastic box of 9mm bullets for the Glock. The pistol was on the table and I planned to slip it in my pocket when we left. For now I pulled back the slide until all the bullets had dropped out and the mag was empty. Then I loaded it again and inserted the mag. I laid out my FDNY jacket and my most comfortable clothes for the next day, and rolled up a light but warm blanket that I strapped to the top of the backpack. I was ready.

One table in the restaurant was covered with sunglasses from the deserted apartments and I walked over and tried a few pairs on. There were other tables with different themes: hats, coats, blankets, batteries and duct tape, weapons. I blamed the last one on Dave, but had to admit I had added a shotgun and a short samurai sword.

What if we come across other survivors – people like us, I mean? Mini asked.

We check out what they know and what they've got, I said. Maybe they've set up camp somewhere.

We should be careful, Anna said. I think we should avoid people if we see them.

In case they're Chasers?

Chasers, whatever. We don't know who or what's out there. Even if there are other survivors, we don't know what they'll be like.

I thought about it. I was sure I'd seen torchlight the previous night. There might be other survivors too; there had to be, sight unseen. What would they be like? There was no sense waiting any longer to find out.

You're right, Anna. We should be careful, I said. Maybe . . . maybe we should work out a few codes, just in case.

Like what? Anna said. She was still sitting at the breakfast table with Dave and Mini, and it was as if the three of them were suddenly looking to me for all the answers. I wished they would get up and help me with the packing.

Like, locations, for a start, I said. We have this place and the Boat Basin, so far. We could call this Site A, and the other Site B. Like, if we're cornered or separated or something, we could yell out, *See you at Site B!*

Can't we think of better names than that? Anna said.

You got any ideas?

We could name them after people we like, she said.

What, so you'd want to call this place Mr Darcy and the Boat Basin Jane Austen?

She shrugged and said: Why not?

Okay, if this is Mr Darcy—

No *way* are we calling this Mr Darcy, Dave said.

Twenty minutes later we'd all written down our choices and put them in a big bowl.

The name we pulled out for 30 Rock was 'Home' and everyone agreed that's what we'd call it from now on. For the Boat Basin we pulled out a piece of paper with the word 'Oprah' written on it. No one would 'fess up to putting that in the bowl and we couldn't tell from the handwriting, but I suspected it might have been Dave.

So, tomorrow we head to the Basin—

Oprah, Dave said.

Right, I went on. Dave, you said there are a few cars along the—

Yeah, there's plenty.

And that they still work and we'll have our choice of—

Yeah, that's what I said.

Right. And we can take Eighth Avenue North – it becomes Central Park West at 59th – and we go all the way up to West 79th?

Dave nodded.

Okay, I said.

I looked at the map – it didn't seem the most direct route but Dave had said the Time Warner Building had collapsed at Columbus Circle, which blocked the way from this direction.

All right, Anna said. So we get a boat and head where? Australia?

Mini laughed.

Boston, Dave said. Hug the coast all the way up. Maybe we'll even spot some survivors on Long Island or somewhere along the way.

You just reminded me, Dave, I said and packed a small pair of binoculars next to the Glock in the side pocket. They were compact but powerful.

All right, so we go down the Hudson River and out Long Island Sound and—

What if there're Chasers near the Boat Basin? Mini asked.

Call it Oprah, Min!

Oh, piss off!

She stood up and scratched at her hair and looked at the floor and then at me.

What if they're there, Jesse? What do we do? I like it here; it's not so bad here, is it?

Min, Dave said, the way was clear—

That was yesterday!

Her voice was louder than I'd ever heard it, and it felt like the voice of reason.

If the Chasers are already there, where do we go? she asked. Is there a Site C? D? Z? What if we're out there and the way's not clear anymore? We need another location like here, a building or something, high above them. Please . . .

I nodded and dipped my hand in the bowl and drew out another little fold of paper. It read 'Mayday'.

I showed it to Mini and in spite of everything she laughed.

All right, guys, I said, looking at the map again. We need a Site C, call-sign Mayday. Some place secure. If you could live in the most secure place in New York, where would you go?

You mean Manhattan?

Yeah, Dave.

Top of Trump Tower.

Really?

What's wrong with that?

Nothing, I said. It's just that yesterday you said the Stock Exchange or the Federal Reserve.

They're all safe.

I checked the map and circled the locations of each of the buildings.

The Woolworth building? I asked. I remembered seeing it near City Hall the day after we'd arrived in New York; it was a big old skyscraper, the type you'd imagine had been built to last.

Fair way away . . .

It'd have good views, though, I went on. And it'd be good to have an option in Lower Manhattan.

It's good, Dave said. Kinda like here.

Fifty-seven storeys tall, I read off the tourist map.

Madison Square Garden?

Too open, I said. Too many ways in.

Times Square, Dave said. M&M World. Maybe a toy store—

Barneys. Shopping all day. That would be a dream.

Yeah, Anna, a real dream, Dave said and he and I rolled our eyes.

We talked like this for ten minutes and in the end had a list of a dozen or so prospects, but we settled on the UN Building. That was Site C; that was our Mayday. It was a fair distance away and in the opposite direction from the Boat Basin, but we decided we might need that kind of escape route.

I looked around at our set-up on the 65th floor and knew that I'd miss this place. I'd miss the quirky areas my friends had created, which showed their different personalities and methods of surviving. It wasn't so bad living here but I knew we had to leave sooner or later, and better to do it on our own terms than to be forced out with no time to prepare.

Dave looked through the weapons he'd stockpiled. I had no idea what kind of gun control they had in New York but it seemed that lots of the apartments below us had a hidden firearm someplace, even some of the offices. Over the past few days I'd learned how to load, operate and un-jam my Glock until I felt I could do it blindfolded. We'd found manuals with some of the guns and Dave said he'd read them cover to cover, although when I looked through one it was quite different from what Dave had described.

The others followed my example and each packed a bag. They were methodical as I had been. Clothes. Food. Water. Fuel. Matches and lighters. Medical kits. A fat wad of cash – ten grand in hundred-dollar bills and a thousand in Euros. If we did make it up the coast or got rescued, we'd be ready.

Do you think the rain washed it all away? The virus in the air, I mean . . . Mini's eyes were wide.

Yeah, I guess, I replied. Maybe it can't live in the cold. But until we know, we shouldn't eat or drink anything out there that may have been exposed. We have to be careful.

How?

I don't know, wash anything we find in bottled water or something.

We don't need anything from outside, Anna said, sitting on the edge of her bed. We've got enough food in this building for months, maybe years. We can always come back here and restock.

There was an awkward pause. I wondered if Dave and Mini were thinking the same as me: that once we left here we could never come back.

I'm gonna do a final sweep of the lower levels, I said. Down to the 59th floor, in case we missed something useful.

Why the gun? Dave asked.

I paused and glanced at the pistol hanging heavily in my right hand. I felt my friends watching me but I didn't bother to justify myself, I just turned and left.

On the 62nd floor there was an apartment owned by a guy called Stuart Hopper; I knew that was his name from the bills lying on his kitchen table. I'd been down here a few times over the past couple of days, helping myself to juice from the fridge and lying on his leather couch reading copies of *Esquire* and *National Geographic*.

I walked through his stainless steel kitchen and went straight to the fish tank. I changed some of the water, cupping out the old and topping it up with bottled. The fish messed around for a while and then I gave them some food, about twice what I'd given them previously. It was all I could do not to make a scene about saying goodbye so I left Stuart Hopper's apartment and headed downstairs.

At the front door of 59C I stood and waited. Waited . . . for what, I don't know. The Glock was in my hand but I couldn't bring myself to pull back the slide and chamber a round. It felt like giving in or something. Giving in to fear, to the stupid, cold, irrational fear that made my arms and shoulders tense up. When a bead of sweat ran down my temple, I decided I'd had enough and pushed open the door with my foot. As it swung inwards I had eyes only for the axed-in area around the handle. I half expected to see the old man who'd lived there standing in the hallway.

But there was nothing unusual. Nothing, until I stepped over the threshold and had the worst case of déjà vu. I had been here before; there was no doubt. I'd seen this room and walked across this floor. Seen the stuffed animals. The layout.

I walked to the study and looked at the desk with the green leather top. There was a typed piece of paper in the typewriter.

We are all storytellers.

We write our stories where and when we can.

This is mine.

I have nothing.

I have everything.

I am alone.

This was the place that had haunted my dream. This was the apartment Dave had said he'd cleared and told me about and warned me to leave alone. I ran a finger along the desk as I scanned the frames on the wall. Newspaper clippings, pictures of politicians, a scene of a coastline, all from an earlier time.

My finger came away dusty; the desk was thick with it. I looked more closely at the typewriter and realised from the fingerprints on the dusty keys that it had recently been used. I had half a memory as I turned and walked down the hallway.

I stood before the door that a couple of days earlier had been locked from the inside. It was almost fully closed but someone had damaged the handle. I reached for it—

Don't.

Dave's voice came from behind me.

Why not? I said.

Because you don't want to go in there.

I want to see it.

You've seen it.

What?

You've seen it. Leave it alone, Jesse.

I looked at Dave closely, then back at the door.

What did I see?

Nothing that you want to see again. Leave it alone.

I want to see for myself.

You don't need to do that.

I want to know.

I want to forget.

You can remember?

I can't forget. It's the tunnel all over again, Jesse. You don't want to see in there. Come on, leave it be.

I turned to Dave but he'd already moved back down the hall. I looked again at the door that screened so much and I knew Dave was right; I had to leave it be. I followed my friend, hoping that all my bad memories would stay behind closed doors once we left this place.

19

How long do you think *it'll be before help arrives?*

The words were written in thick permanent marker on a window in the Rainbow Room. One of us had written it during those first days after we arrived, when we'd expected to see an airlift or convoy heading our way every time we looked at the horizon. I stared beyond the words at the dark clouds rolling in from the east, wondering if it was wrong to hope that Dave's family went in the blink of an eye and were spared any pain when the bombs rained down.

Dave's obsession with survival had moved up a notch with our impending departure from 30 Rock. It was something that was a bit worrying but also kind of funny. That afternoon he trained us how to shoot – we went up to the roof and blasted off hundreds of rounds from the two Glock pistols. At one point I switched to a shotgun but the recoil nearly popped my shoulder out. It did sharpen us up to what we might expect the next day, though. Point, shoot, reload. I didn't flinch at all anymore; I practised until it became almost an automatic response. Point, shoot, reload.

As we left the roof I watched Anna intently. I wanted to be closer to her than I knew I ever could be. My heart was broken and hers wasn't, but I didn't blame her at all.

Guns won't make you safe, you know, she said to no one in particular after we were back in the Rainbow Room. She was obviously still hung up on our target practice.

You think you can kill a hundred of them when they're coming at you? she said. A gun's only good for one thing. It's a way out for the person who's holding it.

I put down my Glock and picked up a comic. I lay on my bed flicking though *Bluntman and Chronic*, wondering why she'd say such a random thing. Was the comment directed at me? Maybe she was reading something deep, some serious piece of literature and it made her imagine the worst. I didn't really want a way out, did I? Or did I subconsciously want her to talk me out of it, to pull me back when I got in too deep?

We're gonna find people when we're in the boat, Dave said. I know it. As soon as we get out of this area, we'll find people.

Maybe we could make it across the Atlantic, Anna said, sounding more optimistic.

Point it home, you mean, I said. Take you all the way back to England in a little boat?

Anna ignored my comment. Did you read that book yet? she asked.

I thought about my answer before speaking.

I've read it before, I said, which was kind of a lie as Dad had read it to me when I was a kid. It was about a boy who was on a lifeboat for months after the ship his family were on sank.

Wasn't the US president going to be in New York the day we were on the subway? Mini asked.

Yeah, so what? Dave said

Wonder if he was here when . . . ?

Doubt it.

What about the rest of the government?

What about it?

You know, when this kind of stuff happens there's always government officials hiding out in a bunker or on a plane or something, Mini said.

And how do you know all this? Anna asked.

Dave cut in before Mini could answer: Computer games, books, movies . . .

Perfect training for the apocalypse, I added.

No doubt, Anna said.

Even if there *are* officials here, so what? I said. So there's some politicians and military out there under a mountain somewhere, with supplies for a hundred years. How's that helping us? How's that keeping us warm when our fuel runs out?

There's plenty of fuel in cars out there, Anna said and I knew where she was going with this.

I'm sick of lugging it up sixty-five flights of stairs, Anna, I said. Look, if you don't want to go—

Then we set up in a house, somewhere with just a couple of floors, Anna said. Somewhere here in New York City – we know this place more than we'll know Boston or wherever we go in a boat. We go to one of those brownstone houses, like in *Sex and the City*.

That's avoiding the bigger issue, Dave said.

Which is?

That we have to get off this friggin' island.

Why, just to take risks?

To see what's out there. Otherwise what are we gonna do – stay here like this for eternity? We gotta get out there and look.

We are, I said. We're going to go to the Boat—

Oprah, said Dave.

I sighed. We're going to *Oprah* tomorrow. It's just . . . Can we believe that there's US government and military people still out there if they haven't shown up here yet? I mean, it's not like this is some backwater . . .

Neither was New Orleans.

This is a bit different, don't you think, Dave? How is it that no one has come along yet?

My dad said governments are good for one thing, Dave said. Taking money and killing people.

Why didn't they prevent this? Why didn't we have any warning?

Shit happens.

Great answer, Dave.

I can't believe they didn't know about this, Mini spoke up. The most advanced government and military in the world? The richest country in the world? How could this happen without warning?

You going back to the CIA conspiracy again, Min? I asked, but I was smiling and the others smiled too.

What if a mosquito bites a Chaser and then bites us – do we get it?

Jesus, Min, I said and we all laughed a little nervously. Let's leave those kinds of questions for the government agents who've conspired in all this when we see them emerge from their bunkers.

We were quiet then, each alone with our thoughts. I kept thinking about the others and wondering what might change between us after tomorrow. I wondered about my family too. Australia was a long way from here so I still clung to my hope that they were okay. But what if whoever had done this decided Australia would be a nice place to attack as well? I imagined my dad and step-mum moving out of their house and living in the streets while an occupying force sat at our dining table eating our food. Then I thought about us, here, living out of other people's apartments, wearing their clothes and eating their food and using their things. Were we that different?

Over dinner we talked again about our decision to leave, and while nothing new came of it I think it helped us all feel better about what we were doing. Deep down, I suspected even Anna knew we had to leave – she admitted we could live here like this for months, but we'd end up taking more risks as our supplies started to run out and were be forced closer to ground level.

One by one we left the dinner table. Dave pottered about with his weapon stash. The girls played Monopoly. I was reading a novel that Anna had recommended,

The Life of Pi. Dad had read it to me when I was about eight or nine. I think it was the final book he'd read to me, the last experience I had of being read to aloud. By page forty I realised how much I missed the sound of his voice. My mum's voice too, singing me to sleep.

I think the girls noticed something was up with me because they packed away their game and got into their beds and Anna said: Can you read some to us?

I looked at her and Mini, then over at Dave, who'd stopped reading his own book – *Modern Counter-insurgency Techniques and Urban Warfare in the Middle East: Lessons Learned* – and I nodded.

Dave poured himself a Coke and went to lounge in his recliner by the windows to the east.

Okay, I said. To set the scene, our young protagonist, the boy named Pi, is adrift in the ocean—

How old is he? asked Dave.

Sixteen.

Like us! Mini said.

Yeah, I replied. Anyway, he's Indian, like sub-continent or Asian Indian, not Native American Indian. Anyway, his family owned a zoo in India but they sold up to go live in Canada. They were on a ship with some of their animals, heading to their new land, when the ship went down. Pi was the only human to survive.

Only human? Mini asked.

He's on a lifeboat. There's also a zebra, a hyena, an orangutan, and a Bengal tiger named Richard Parker.

What's the ape's name?

I'm not sure if orangutans are apes, Anna said.

I think they are, Mini said.

Wikipedia would settle this, Dave joked and we laughed.

Anyway, her name is Orange Juice.

I read them fifty pages that night, by which time I was the only one awake. I put the book on the floor, switched off the little battery lamp, and turned over to sleep.

At home when I couldn't sleep I would think about all the things I'd done that I wished I could take back. Embarrassing things, like making a fool of myself in class, or laughing so hard at my friend's fifth birthday party that I wet my pants. Stupid things, like crashing Dad's car into the fence, or stealing a pencil case from a supermarket, or egging my neighbour's house and getting caught. But those things didn't worry me anymore. In fact, now I cherished those memories.

I thought about everything that had happened since we'd come to 30 Rock.

I'm a part of this, I realised; I'm part of this war. I'm a murderer and a thief. I've taken possessions and life and I feel more guilt-free than I should.

Goodnight, Mini whispered into the darkness.

Goodnight.

20

When the others got up for breakfast the next day, I stayed in bed. Memories from my nightmare still lingered and I burrowed deep under my two doonas, trying to push the images away. Through the small opening near my head I could see that Dave was ready to go, his gun locked and loaded.

Stove's out of gas, Anna said. Can we use the generator to boil a kettle?

Generator's out of gas, Dave said.

I don't understand why you Americans call petrol 'gas', she said. You call gas 'gas' but why call petrol 'gas'?

They argued for a while, more about her acerbic views of American culture than anything else. The argument ended with Dave saying: Well, at least you don't have

to worry about us Americans anymore. Then he fell
silent. I still didn't get out of bed.

What are we doing? Anna said about an hour later.
We're leaving today, aren't we?

I guessed that Mini was still asleep because I hadn't
heard her voice. I watched the doors to the kitchen,
and for the first time I wished someone other than one
of my friends would come through those doors. Even a
Chaser would do, someone different, someone—

Are you going to come with us? Anna asked. She
was sitting on the end of my bed. We're going today.

I didn't reply. I pretended I was still asleep, but I
knew she'd know I wasn't. I was tired and confused and
I couldn't be bothered with the unknown today.

It's really selfish of you, you know? she said.

I felt heat rise up my neck and it hurt when I
swallowed. Maybe I was getting tonsillitis. I felt sweaty,
my heart raced, I couldn't close my eyes tightly enough.
Couldn't help come to me? Couldn't we stay just a little
bit longer?

We've got everything planned and ready and now
you're being stupid, she said. This was mostly your
idea.

She got up and went into the kitchen but still I
lay in bed. I stayed like that all day. I could hear the

others moving about and getting ready and occasionally one would come over and try to convince me to get up but I didn't move. They could go without me for all I cared. I would make my own life without them and who knows, maybe I'd be all right, after all.

Finally, when it was getting dark, I got out of bed. The others weren't around but their bags were still there so I knew they hadn't left. I grabbed a Sprite from the bar and headed up to the observation decks still wrapped in my bedding. I wanted to avoid the others. I felt selfish but I didn't care. My throat felt like it was on fire so maybe I really was sick. Or maybe I was just losing my nerve. I drank my can of drink, looked to the south and west and sat there – watching, waiting, drinking. I could have stayed there like that for days. Maybe I was becoming one of them: a Chaser.

The night sky was clear, the inky black above me full of stars. It reminded me of camping as a kid and sleeping out in the open on hot summer nights and counting shooting stars. The darker it was, the more stars you'd see. And right then I thought that this city was probably the darkest place on earth. The ground that stretched out before me, once full of light and life, was now a dark shadow. It was almost as if things had been inverted, and the carpet of lights in the sky was making up for what had gone from below.

Then, to the west, in what I knew was New Jersey beyond the Hudson River, a number of blocks lit up. Power.

I had never seen something man-made that was as beautiful as that patchwork of streetlights, nor had I cried that hard since I was a kid thinking about my mother.

Beautiful, glorious, deliberate: *power.*

I was ready to leave.

21

New Jersey, represent! Dave yelled. Yee-ha!

Maps were checked. Decisions were made. We were riding high.

We take a boat across the Hudson and then it's only a few blocks from the shore to where the lights are on, I said. Imagine – they might all be fine over there!

They might have news.

They might have answers.

They might have aeroplanes.

We smiled and laughed and ate through a decent chunk of our table-load of fine boxed chocolates. We decided to leave at first light; we'd be in New Jersey by lunchtime. I felt happy to be alive and I didn't feel guilty for delaying my friends anymore, not one little bit. They treated me like an explorer. I was Cook or

Columbus or Polo; I'd discovered something and it wasn't just a new land, it was proof of life. Our new earth was bigger than just me, bigger than us.

Our conversation jumped all over the place. We were too hyped up to stick to one topic.

I'm going to drive a fire truck around, Mini said and I suspected she was a little bit drunk.

I saw an episode of *Cribs* on MTV once, Dave said. This rapper had a garage and you expected him to have, like, a collection of Ferraris and Porsches, but all he had in there were fire trucks – just because he could!

I hate MTV and that's obscene, Anna said. There are kids starving in the world.

Hate's a strong word, I said.

What, you've never hated anything? I thought you Aussies hated us Brits.

I looked at her in shock. If Anna had got the sense that I hated her, she had my intentions all wrong.

We don't hate you guys at all, I said. We still share the same Queen. It's Dave here; his countrymen fought you guys for independence. He's the hater.

Damn straight, Dave said. And we'll whoop anyone's ass that tries to come over here and do shit like that again.

What, colonise?

Whatever, he said. You've seen the apartments and offices below us, almost everyone in America is carrying. If any other nation tries landing here, there'll be consequences – three hundred million armed Americans ready to rock.

Imagine what the US would have been like without the Louisiana Purchase? I said. Napoleon may have retreated back here and retooled and rearmed his forces and taken another crack at the Brits.

See, you do hate us, Anna said, staring out the window.

Anyway, I said, maybe there aren't starving kids to worry about anymore.

Maybe it's even worse now.

Yeah, maybe . . . I said and looked out at the lights in New Jersey. But maybe we won't have to worry about global warming anymore.

We were silent, thinking about the implications of a new time for which none of us had the answers. I hoped we'd soon be with people who knew more than we did, who knew what had been going on around the world. I'd grown up with the internet; I was used to finding out about things as soon as they happened. To be left in the dark, as we had been for the past ten days, felt surreal. Finding out who was behind this didn't seem to matter much anymore; it was the consequences of what they'd done that were important. Soon we'd be in New Jersey, talking to real live people, finding out what the future might hold.

I looked at the others around the table, each lost in their own thoughts. No matter what, no matter who we met tomorrow, I'd always be grateful to my three friends. I hoped we'd stay friends. We made a good team, but I wondered whether we would have formed such a strong unit if all this had never happened. I guessed I would never know.

22

We stayed up all night. I tried to sleep at about 3 am, but I couldn't close my eyes for more than a few seconds for fear the lights of New Jersey would blink out. They stayed on. They stayed on and at 5 am we decided to make our move. I had one last look around the place that had sheltered us, before the others filed out and I shut the door. With my big pack on, I led the way downstairs, a torch in each hand to illuminate the dark stairwell. We emerged in the lobby and out onto Rockefeller Plaza, beating the first rays of the sun.

On 47th Street there were still the fire engines and police cars, just as I'd remembered them. The air was biting and I put on my FDNY jacket against the cold. Rather than heading out towards Eighth Avenue and then north to 79th Street guided only by torchlight, we decided to sit in the cab of one of the fire engines and wait for the sun to come up. The battery was flat so we couldn't turn the heater on, but we blew into our hands and huddled together to keep warm.

At the first hint of sunrise we got out of the cab and checked the small map I kept folded away in my jacket pocket. We made our way west a couple of blocks and turned right onto Eighth Avenue. I asked Dave a few times if this car or that one were the ones he'd started up when he did his trip, but he just said he couldn't remember. I started to get annoyed with him; he was the only one who'd taken this route before. I should have told him to lift a wiper or make some other mark on the cars, like I'd done on my trip. We wasted a lot of time trying to get different cars started, with no luck for three blocks. Some were locked, many didn't have keys, some had flat batteries, and a few had dead people in them.

I sat in an SUV and turned the key in the ignition – nothing.

Gee, Dave, I called out through the window. Lucky we're not relying on you to—

I stopped and didn't move. Six Chasers had walked around the corner of the block up ahead. They looked like walking ghosts, sapped of energy, six lonely shells of human beings shuffling along. They stopped at a small crater that was full of water and knelt and drank. They could have been a herd of animals.

I glanced at Dave and the girls who were on the other side of the street. They quickly crouched down behind a taxi. So far we hadn't been spotted but if they continued this way—

One of the Chasers stood and walked in our direction.

I slid down in my seat and held my breath. When I looked out through the bottom of the windscreen, the Chaser had stopped to pick up some slushy snow. He ate it as he continued on.

Dave motioned to me and mouthed, *Gun!* but I shook my head.

I looked past the lone figure coming our way and saw that his friends had got to their feet and were walking in our direction too. Six Chasers, coming towards us. Some had dried blood on them but they didn't look injured.

The first guy was now twenty metres away. I stayed still; I was sure if I moved he'd notice and make a beeline for me.

Suddenly one of the Chasers in the group made a noise – a weird high-pitched monkey sound – and the others stopped and responded by making the same sound in unison. Then the one closest to us turned and walked back towards his group but he slipped on some ice and fell hard. His friends watched on with interest.

I was transfixed, and when the fallen man got back to his feet, he half-turned and looked my way and I panicked and moved just a little—

His eyes went wide when he saw me. I noticed that his face was grazed and he had blood dripping from his forehead. He turned to his group but before he could make a noise, they were on him like animals; they pinned him to the ground and drank and drank.

I looked to my friends but they had already made a move. I crawled out of the open door of the SUV and headed back the way we'd come, using the vehicle as cover. When I reached the intersection at the end of the street, I crossed the road on my hands and knees behind a massive pile-up of cars. I hoped and prayed I wasn't being followed, expecting at any moment to feel a live weight on my back. I crawled as fast as I could across the snow-covered bitumen, grazing my hands, my face and neck flaming with fear. I was going to be attacked, my blood would be drunk, I would die slowly and in pain as mouths closed on me and—

My friends were behind the corner of a building and they waved me towards them like sirens calling a lost seaman to shore. I reached them and sank against the smooth wall of the building, closing my eyes because if the Chasers were coming I didn't want to see. I felt like throwing up but I took deep breaths through my panic and after a few minutes I was brave enough to open my eyes and look at the world.

My friends were silent, watching me. Why hadn't they waited? They didn't try to explain or console me, maybe because they didn't know what to say. Dave stared at his feet. Mini looked like she was someplace else, and Anna looked from one to the other, like she was appealing to them to help me. My hands were bloody and raw and cold and I couldn't believe I hadn't thought to wear gloves. I clenched my fists and stood up and led the way west, towards Tenth Avenue.

My friends kept watching me as we walked. I couldn't look at them, couldn't meet their eyes. I led them into a cafe, entering through the smashed remnants of a window. I took off my backpack and found the medical kit. I washed my hands with bottled water, then applied antiseptic and wrapped each hand in a bandage. It reminded me of being in the arcade when Anna had tended the cut on my forehead, but she didn't offer to help this time, just watched. They were all watching me, waiting for a sign. Waiting for me to show them the way.

When my hands were bandaged I put on my pack and led them back out to the street. It was snowing and the light powder coated my head and shoulders as we turned north onto Tenth.

We stopped at each intersection and looked carefully around corners. There were more pile-ups here and the streets at West 54th and Tenth were impassable. The Glock was heavy in my jacket pocket and my pack weighed me down as I trudged on, weaving though the stationary gridlock of smashed and abandoned vehicles. We headed east and then left onto Ninth Avenue.

The others were still following me and I was drawn into a building near the junction of West 59th Street, where smoke was billowing from one of the windows. We went slowly, leaving our backpacks at the door. It was dark inside so I retrieved the torch and flicked it on. Its weak beam lit the space but there was nothing to see; the building ended where it began. Inside there were piles of rubble and not much else – it was like the place had been gutted by a demolition team, like a bomb had gone off leaving only the outer shell.

There was no one there but I didn't want to find anyone. The smoke we'd seen from outside was coming from a few small fires amongst the piles of rubble, remnants of upper levels that were now open to the sky; an artificial atrium.

I went back to the doorway where I could sit and watch the street while remaining hidden. None of us said anything. Whether we were in shock or it was something else, I didn't know. We were alone in our own minds.

Screw this town! Screw this town and what's left of it!

Anna and Mini looked at me. They had tears on their cheeks.

You didn't go to the Boat Basin, did you, Dave.

He didn't answer. Didn't have to. It wasn't a question.

I know you didn't, and if you say you did but you can't remember anything about the journey then you're a liar, you hear me? You understand?

He nodded, slowly. Tears.

I don't care if we part ways here, I said. I really don't. I'll make it to the Boat Basin on my own and you three can do whatever you want. I never asked you to stay with me all this time. I never said I didn't want to be alone. I'm used to being alone. I've been alone most of my life. It's nothing new, so believe me, you three can leave and I won't blame you or waste time wondering why.

I left them at the doorway and walked back inside, amongst the rubble, scratching myself on the fractured concrete walls. I saw some bloated bodies in the wreckage and felt nothing. I didn't know who I was anymore. I was tired and none of my friends could help me and I wanted to be alone. I leaned against a wall and cried until snot was streaming from my nose. I stayed there, sobbing, until I couldn't cry any longer; I could only make pathetic whimpering noises. The sound made me angry and I squeezed my fists and kicked the wall, kicked it with all the strength I had left.

When I finally walked back to the doorway, my friends were gone. I felt numb. I picked up my backpack as if on autopilot and strapped it on, fastening the waistband so it wouldn't rattle around if I had to run. I put the torch away and held my Glock and walked out onto the street.

Mini, Anna and Dave were standing there. They looked strong, confident; they looked how I wanted to feel.

I chambered a round in the Glock.

I'm going, I said. We're going to make it to the Boat Basin, no matter what. Whatever it takes, I will be in a boat and in New Jersey by the end of today. Whatever it takes.

23

Dave walked ahead this time and I felt more confident now, like he was shouldering some of the burden. Navigating the deserted streets was still frightening; every corner held an unseen threat and the dark shopfronts looked menacing.

When we were a block south of Central Park, we hid out in an empty cafe while about two dozen Chasers walked past at a snail's pace. They looked weaker than the previous group and were all ages, from early teens to old men. Like the others we'd seen that day, they were dressed against the cold and I guessed they must have been caught outdoors when the city was attacked. It made me sad to think that the only difference between us and them was that we'd been underground at the right time. The group moved like they had no energy and their faces were without hope; it was all I could do not to go out and give them bottles of drink from the cafe's fridges. But I stayed hidden. I was only sixteen. Self-preservation is the downside of being in a position of advantage.

Looks like they've gone, Dave said, peering out of the cafe's windows.

Can't we stay and rest for a bit more? Mini asked. Just for a bit?

Sure, I replied and we did. We sat there and stretched out and I drank a Coke and enjoyed the sugar rush. We'd walked only a kilometre. Maybe two. I felt like I'd run a marathon. Every step had been like navigating a war zone, where someone could kill you at any moment. We'd had to dogleg east and north, then west and then north again, close to Central Park, the place we wanted to avoid.

New Jersey, huh . . . I said, and Dave replied: Yeah, New Jersey.

No one seemed to want to talk but I felt we needed to so I said: I'm looking forward to a shower. A long, hot shower.

To have a proper hair wash, Anna agreed.

To shave.

I miss TV.

I laughed at Mini's call.

Yeah, I miss TV too.

As they talked I watched them closely and it was interesting to see how much they'd changed since that subway ride. How much we'd all changed.

Dave had probably altered the most, especially since he'd got back from his day and a half outside. He'd walked the streets of New York alone and I didn't know what he'd done while he was away and I didn't want to know. I could imagine well enough. Maybe he'd just sat in a fire engine or a shop and cried. Why did it even bother me where he'd been for all that time? Whatever he was doing, it was his business and I didn't want to ask because that would be prying, like asking Anna what she wrote in her journal or Mini about her thoughts. All I knew is that he'd come back different – he'd changed. Maybe he'd seen death on a biblical scale, like me.

Anna had taken out her notebook and was writing in it, and I loved that even in the midst of all this she was doing her own thing. I hoped she was creating a story to take her to another place far away from here. It was what she deserved. As she wrote, she bit her lip in concentration and I thought I could smell strawberries. Her lips were red and her eyelashes long and dark and

I watched her writing and wished I could kiss her again. I never would, would I?

And Mini. Mini had grown to be my favourite. She was always there but never in the way; she was economical and giving and reserved and generous, all at the same time. She looked at me sometimes, I knew. The kind of looks I gave Anna. I'd seen her do it at the UN camp and I knew she liked me. Thinking about that now made my cheeks and ears burn. I didn't want to be a teenager anymore and I didn't want to be here anymore; I was sick of living in my head and thinking too much. I wanted to be older and stronger and have more answers than my friends could provide.

Let's go in five, I said and they agreed.

I walked out to the bathroom and a couple of rats scurried away. I went to wash my face but there was no water. Just ash in the hand-basin and a big burn mark on one wall and I stared at myself in the broken mirror and replayed my nightmare in full. I'm standing in an open pasture. I see little glimpses, little flashes until suddenly I'm seeing myself from above. I'm standing in Central Park, but I'm not alone. I'm surrounded. By Chasers. They want what I have. They want what pumps inside me and I know I must give it up. I have no fight left in me. There's blood on my arms and it drips freely down to the earth. I close my eyes, put my hands in the air and yell at them to take me. My scream for them echoes and fades and when I open my eyes I can see that they haven't moved. They watch me, like I've watched them so many times. They move in a giant circle, like a great sea of fish cycloning out of the way of a predator. Maybe they fear me like I fear them?

I coughed and spat out dusty mucus in the basin. My eyes watered, tears fell and I felt a breeze and was startled from my thoughts.

Mini was there, standing behind me in the open doorway.

You're not alone, she said. No matter what your dream says. You're okay.

I stared at her. How could she know about my dream? I hadn't told anyone. I didn't understand what was going on but I was grateful to Mini; in some ways she knew so much more than the others. Would I ever be able to properly thank her for getting me through all this?

Thanks, I said. I looked at myself in the dirty mirror and turned away and left the room with her.

I didn't mean to bother you. I'm fine, really.

She didn't speak but she nodded that she understood, and she did – more than anyone else ever could.

I put on my heavy backpack and the others followed me outside. The snow had stopped and the sun was bright now, the clouds sparse, and there was hope in the air.

This way, I said and led north to the end of the block, until we reached Columbus Circle, where Broadway and Central Park South and West 58th Street all collide. The area was vast and open, empty of life but full of wrecked cars and broken buildings. I strode across the road, weaving my way through the chaos. I wanted to continue west along Broadway but it was an impassable mountain of shattered buildings. I changed tack and led the others down Central Park West until it too became impassable. I crouched behind a bus that shielded me from the park and checked my map.

Why are we stopped? Anna asked.

We're going to have to go through the park.

No way.

Uh uh, Dave said.

Look, the only alternative is to go back the way we've come, and try another way south and west to get around all this.

Let's do that then.

It'll waste the entire day, maybe more, I said. And it might be blocked as well. We know the park is clear. We head north, and we can get back onto the road a couple of blocks past all this mess and head west.

I don't like it, Anna said.

We'll be careful.

It's dangerous.

We'll be quiet.

Please, no.

Dave?

He's right, Anna. It's the only way.

But we know they're in there, Anna said. We've seen them, we've watched them from the Top of the Rock. They're near all the water in the ponds.

We'll just go round the edge, stick clear of the paths—

There's thousands of them in there, Jesse!

I felt sick.

Look, we do this or we go back and try the other route another day. The park today, or the unknown tomorrow.

She was silent. Dave was silent. It was Mini's quiet voice I heard.

We should go through the park. We should go and we should do it now.

24

The south-west corner of Central Park was deserted. We tried to stick to the perimeter but as the undergrowth became denser we were forced further in. We crossed a wide, empty plain; the frosty grass that peeked through the snow in patches was as slippery as glass. My blood turned to ice as I realised this was the place of my nightmare. This was the open expanse where the mass of Chasers had circled around me and watched me, thirsty for my blood.

Walking through the streets seemed preferable now. I missed those man-made canyons and their reminders of what had once been. This was far scarier. Empty, desolate. Windy. I imagined ten thousand pairs of eyes burning into me. The trees here were alive with them, I could feel it. Without speaking, we broke into a half run. My feet skidded but I didn't fall; I wouldn't fall—

I slipped and came down hard on the icy ground. I got back up and kept going. The Chasers would be on me soon, I knew it. The sun had disappeared behind the clouds and it started snowing and I ran hard now.

A noise startled me. A foreign noise; a noise I hadn't heard for over a week.

I stopped running and squinted up at the sky. There were clear patches, despite the heavy cloud bank that had rolled in and hung low and littered the ground with snow. My breath fogged in front of me and I felt dizzy and I fell again, then got to my feet and kept running, looking at the sky, listening.

I pinpointed the noise. It came from a place high above me and off to the east. Four small jet aircraft flew in a diamond formation from north to south, faint lines of vapour in their wake. They were far from the centre of the city and didn't seem to be flying towards it. Why would they give this place such a wide berth? I waved my hands over my head as they doubled back and flew east over Long Island.

Come back! I called to them. Come back! Come back . . .

I looked at the others. I could tell they felt the same way I did but we didn't have time to cry about it now.

Come on, I said. Move!

We ran and a new noise came and it was terrifying. Dozens of Chasers emerged from the trees and started running for us. We headed west and sprinted over a road and I looked over my shoulder—

The Chasers were only two hundred metres or so behind us. Unlike the poor infected souls we'd seen earlier that day, these Chasers looked strong and purposeful. I looked forward again and kept running and knew I'd have to dump my pack if they gained on me. These weren't just desperate, opportunistic Chasers; these were the kind that drank people because they could.

Run harder! Dave yelled and it was like he was yelling straight into my ear and I ran as fast as I could. I was puffing hard. I remembered that Mini had asthma and realised with a shock that I'd forgotten to bring her the ventilator refill she'd asked for when I went out that day. I looked back and saw she was falling behind. This was it. This would be the moment when I had to stand tall.

Come on, guys! I yelled, and they seemed to push themselves a little harder and we crossed the road and followed West 67th Street that would lead us out of the park.

More Chasers. About twenty of them, huddled around a fire in a car park up ahead. They looked weak and some of them watched me running, but they didn't seem interested in chasing – just watching.

A familiar face was among them. I almost tripped over the kerb but got my footing back and turned to look at them again as I ran past. A familiar face watched me, stared right back at me—

The boy.

The boy I'd met many blocks from here, at the East River. The boy I had given a bottle of water and an apple.

He was drinking now, from a water bottle. Not the bottle I'd given him but another – this group were all drinking from bottles. They looked like Chasers but they had fire in a steel drum and they drank from bottles.

I kept running, but when I looked back they did the most unexpected thing. The boy, then two others, waved at me. They waved at me as I disappeared from view into the chaos of Central Park West.

They'd waved.

They'd waved at me. I will never know if it was a wave hello or a wave goodbye, but they'd been drinking from bottles and they had a fire and they'd waved.

25

We were followed all along West 67th Street. Pursued by Chasers who were at least as fast as us and didn't seem to be tiring. Chased over Columbus Avenue where I skidded to a hard stop against a yellow school bus and turned right, ignoring the sharp pain in my arm, heading north up Columbus. It was twelve blocks to 79th Street. Twelve blocks north and then three blocks west to the Boast Basin.

I heard squealing being me and looked back at an intersection about a hundred metres away; one of the Chasers had slipped and the others were already upon her, drinking her as she lived and screamed.

I'd only stopped for a second or two but in that moment I recognised another face. It didn't register until I was running again, weaving my way between parked cars, the image flashing into my memory like a hot, sharp knife. We couldn't stop running, we ran for our lives, but I remembered one of the Chasers behind me. It was the guy I'd seen from the Top of the Rock, the one I'd watched drinking from a dead body. I looked over my shoulder; my friends were right behind me and the Chasers were beyond them but they were a blur of strangers. Maybe I'd just imagined that face?

I slipped and fell on the icy ground. I could hear Dave urging the others to keep going as I got to my feet. Anna watched ahead but Mini looked back at me and called my name.

Left! I yelled, and Dave led the way down West 68th Street. It was clear enough to get through and we ran fast and rounded the next right, and then we were on Broadway which would take us all the way to the Boat Basin.

Wait!

What? Dave said as he came up next to me. We kept running but our paced had slowed.

You guys take the next left!

What about—

I'll head straight down Broadway and they won't see you, only me and—

We're not separating! Anna yelled, and we ran faster, skirting behind three abandoned garbage trucks that cut across the lanes and around a crater filled with taxis. A car door was stuck deep into the road and we had to hurdle over it.

Go left! I yelled to Dave, and he turned the corner of West 73rd Street.

Mini was panting for breath and Anna was close to me and I yelled to them:

Go! Run into a building and wait for five minutes then head west.

We're not separating!

I looked behind me. I couldn't see the Chasers but they wouldn't have been more than a few hundred metres back and they were surely closing in on us.

I'll meet you at the—

Don't—

I'll meet you at Oprah!

No!

Dave kept running but I knew he got it, and when Mini realised what I meant the tears started streaming down her cheeks.

Hide for five and then head straight there, I said as we ran. Wait here until they've all chased after me . . .

No! Anna said. She turned and looked at me like she'd never looked at me before and I knew, in that moment, she loved me.

I can outrun them. I can outrun them, but if we stay together you might slow me down and then we'll all get caught, so you just wait here for a while, okay?

What if it doesn't work?

It'll work. I'll meet you there.

What if they get you?

They won't catch me, I'm fast.

I unclipped my backpack and slid it off, removing the big FDNY jacket at the same time. I looked like I was about to run a circuit on the track. I didn't bother with a gun; there were too many of them so it would only be good for one thing and I wasn't interested in that.

But—

No buts. Sorry, Anna, Min. I have to do this.

Mini nodded and Dave pulled her back into a shop and Anna looked from them to me like she couldn't believe they were letting me do this.

What if you get lost?

I know the way.

What if you forget?

I can't forget.

What if you don't make it?

I have to make it. You three are all I have.

She nodded and sucked back her tears and I reached for her but she took a step closer to Mini and Dave in the dark shop.

I'll be waiting there for you.

I know, I said.

Then I turned and saw a group of Chasers round onto Broadway and I faced them and screamed as loud as I could, out in the middle of the street. They saw me and ran harder, and I ripped the bandages off my hands and showed them blood. I waved at them and they were chasing me now, only me.

I ran up Broadway, through the gaps between cars and over bodies and I thought about those Chasers in the car park who hadn't chased but had waved and—

I risked one last look over my shoulder and saw that my friends were in the clear. I knew that no matter what I couldn't outrun my pursuers, but maybe, just maybe, I could make it to a car and get in and lock the doors and drive away.

The Basin was five blocks away and I ran as fast as I'd run that day when I'd first fled for my life. I felt my heart pumping blood through my veins and I thought of my friends and the group of Chasers who'd waved and I knew one thing, at the very least: I was not alone.

I ran like I was never coming back and wondered, Would my friends be there? Would I see them again? Of course I would, I thought, why wouldn't I? I remembered a girl back home who spoke in class sometimes when we were meant to be silent. Spoke to people who weren't there. All year they made her see a psychologist and she was silent after that but never the same, like she'd forgotten how to smile.

I wanted to be on a houseboat that could float down the river and into the harbour and beyond to the ocean. I didn't care if I couldn't steer it; I'd be happy if it made its own way and the current took me wherever it pleased. I'd like that actually. I'd like to let go and not have to worry about anything, not have to be the one steering the boat or anything else in life. I wanted to close my eyes and drift.

A subway sign flashed by. I thought of my friends. I remembered the banging and the fire and the man who fell like a tree when he was shot, silent, slowly, hitting the ground as gently as an angel falling on the snow.

I glanced back for my friends but I couldn't see them; they weren't there. I ran. I thought about the subway ride we'd taken that day. When my world had rocked and turned sideways; hot, black, lonely.

I thought about coming to in the cold darkness. I'd emerged from under an upturned seat. I'd fumbled around blindly and found Anna's backpack and in it her torch and, with its light, my friends. I'd seen the vacant forms of Dave and Anna and Mini as they lay there together: silent, broken.

My broken friends.

They had been with me the whole time, but only I had seen them after that day. Only I *could* see them. They had done for me what I could not do for myself. I'd been the one to vomit up chocolate cake and look longingly to the east. I had shot a man dead in the street – he'd fallen like a tree. I was the one who broke through the locked door in 59C and used the typewriter in the study.

Blood stained my hands; I'd seen everything.

Only I had climbed out of that subway tunnel.

Dave had never finished that joke; I never heard how it ended. I'd made it to 30 Rock and remembered Dave talking about the observation deck as I climbed the stairs, alone. I'd made myself breakfast and kept myself company. I heard their voices clearly at first, but soon their activities took over and clouded them, and I knew I was losing them long before I decided to leave 30 Rock. I'd ruffled their beds and served them food and pretended not to notice when I scraped it away, like I pretended not to notice so much else. I sat there on the observation decks and took it in shifts by myself. There were no other survivors from that subway crash and none that I'd met since and there may never be. Just me and the Chasers and the hint of those I'd seen from afar.

I was alone.

I could admit that now; I was no longer afraid to. I wondered if someone would ask me about it one day and whether they'd say there was nothing wrong with imaginary friends as long as I knew they weren't real. But my friends had been real, once. Who's to say that every bit of them had to leave when they died? Some head doctor might tell me otherwise one day, but even then I'd be glad just for the chance to talk about them. And good luck to anyone who tries to pry my friends away from me; they're not going to civilise them out of me, not ever.

I was alone but I was not by myself. As I ran and hid and evaded the Chasers, I knew that more than ever. The days would become clearer and longer and the sun would shine again soon, hot and hard and bright like it did back home. I knew my friends were with me, the same way I knew my family were with me. No matter what happened now, no matter where I went or what I found, there were other voices that travelled with me. Faces too. Laughter. Opinions. Sadness and desires. They were all there inside me when I really needed them.

Wet snow fell. There was a breeze. I ran.

I was on my own but I was not alone.

I was capable of anything. Everything. I couldn't forget.

I rounded a corner and ran into a stone building that was as dark as a cave and there was silence behind me as I ran up the fire stairs and out onto the top floor and I ran to the window and watched the Chasers on the street below trying to figure out where I'd gone and I took a step back and looked at my reflection in the window.

'I am alone.'

The story continues in

SURVIVOR

The thrilling next instalment from the Alone Series

Acknowledgements

Special thanks are due to those who have been invaluable and integral to this project seeing the light of day. I had unwavering support from my three families: Beasley, Wallace, and Phelan. My brothers Sam and Jesse were perfect target readers, and I stole a good name, as I did with Anna and Min Pei. To Emily, Andrew, Michelle, Tony and Natasha, thanks for your encouragement. Thanks to Alex Robotham and her parents Viv and Mike, pro readers and hosts extraordinaire. My agents at Curtis Brown, Writers House, and UTA, particularly Pippa Masson, Victoria Gutierrez, Stephanie Thwaites, Josh Getzler, Kassie Evashevski and Yuli Masinovsky, provided razor-sharp feedback and resolute faith in my work. The editorial team at Hachette, Fiona Hazard, Tegan Morrison and Kate Ballard, have been outstanding and understanding in dealing with this author who has been so protective of his new baby. Nicole Wallace, as always, was my muse and rock.

James Phelan was born in 1979 and lives in Melbourne. He studied and worked in architecture before turning to English literature and graduating with a Master of Arts in writing, which he used to waste five good years at a newspaper. His first non-fiction book was published at 25 and he has been a full-time novelist since 2006. He is currently dividing his time between writing adult thrillers and the post-apocalyptic Alone Series for young adults.